HOLE CARD

Trudy Deakens was asking for trouble playing stud poker with Bert Tooney. But there was no stopping her from going after the horse Tooney had filched from her.

Skye Fargo saw Trudy's face fall when Tooney flipped the ace that beat her. "I win the horse, the money, and I'm gonna take your little ass, too," Tooney gloated.

"Not the way I see it," Fargo cut in.

"Who the hell are you?" Tooney growled.

"Somebody who likes an honest game," Fargo said.

Tooney went for his gun, but Fargo's Colt was out and firing before Tooney had cleared his holster. Tooney's long body folded forward almost in two as the heavy bullet ripped through him.

"You coming?" Fargo asked Trudy, as he wondered how much more gunfire it would take to make her use some sense. . . .

THE TRAILSMAN RIDES ON

☐ **THE TRAILSMAN #79: SMOKY HELL TRAIL by Jon Sharpe.** Through a blizzard of bullets and a cloud of gunsmoke . . . with a kid he aimed to turn into a man . . . with a lady he aimed to turn into a woman . . . and wave after wave of killers he had to aim fast to turn into corpses . . . Skye Fargo rides the desolate stretch of savage wilderness they call the Smoky Hell Trail. (154045—$2.75)

☐ **THE TRAILSMAN #82: MESCALERO MASK by Jon Sharpe.** On a special investigative mission, Skye has to blaze through a tangle of rampaging redskin terror and two-faced, kill-crazy bluecoats to keep the U.S. flag from being soaked in blood and wrapped around his bullet-ridden corpse . . . (156110—$2.95)

☐ **THE TRAILSMAN #83: DEAD MAN'S FOREST by Jon Sharpe.** When a lady friend is taken hostage, Skye Fargo sets out to hunt down a killer and gets caught in a tangle of sex, salvation and slaying. He soon finds out too much of a good thing can kill a man. . . . (156765—$2.95)

☐ **THE TRAILSMAN #84: UTAH SLAUGHTER by Jon Sharpe.** Skye Fargo rides a road to hell paved with rampaging renegades and lusting ladies. This was Utah, where a man could have as many women as he could satisfy and as much trouble as he could handle . . . and the Trailsman was setting records for both. . . . (157192—$2.95)

☐ **THE TRAILSMAN #85: CALL OF THE WHITE WOLF by Jon Sharpe.** When Skye Fargo led the wagon train organized by beautiful Annabel Dorrance into the mountains of Montana, he figured there'd be redskins, outcast bands ready to rape and pillage, and the occasional tussle with Annabel's trigger-happy boyfriend—but he never thought he'd meet a fearsome tooth-and-nail killer! (157613—$2.95)

Buy them at your local bookstore or use this convenient coupon for ordering.

NEW AMERICAN LIBRARY
P.O. Box 999, Bergenfield, New Jersey 07621

Please send me the books I have checked above. I am enclosing $_____
(please add $1.00 to this order to cover postage and handling). Send check or money order—no cash or C.O.D.'s. Prices and numbers are subject to change without notice.

Name_____

Address_____

City _____ State _____ Zip Code _____
Allow 4-6 weeks for delivery.
This offer, prices and numbers are subject to change without notice.

THE TRAILSMAN 89

TARGET CONESTOGA

by

Jon Sharpe

A SIGNET BOOK

NEW AMERICAN LIBRARY

A DIVISION OF PENGUIN BOOKS USA INC.

PUBLISHER'S NOTE

This book is a work of fiction. Names, characters, places, and incidents either are the product of the author's imagination or are used fictitiously, and any resemblance to actual persons, living or dead, events, or locales is entirely coincidental.

The first chapter of this book previously appeared in *Mexican Massacre*, the eighty-eighth book in this series.

The Trailsman

Beginnings . . . they bend the tree and they mark the man. Skye Fargo was born when he was eighteen. Terror was his midwife, vengeance his first cry. Killing spawned Skye Fargo, ruthless, cold-blooded murder. Out of the acrid smoke of gunpowder still hanging in the air, he rose, cried out a promise never forgotten.

The Trailsman, they began to call him, all across the West: searcher, scout, hunter, the man who could see where others only looked, his skills for hire but not his soul, the man who lived each day to the fullest, yet trailed each tomorrow. Skye Fargo, the Trailsman, the seeker who could take the wildness of a land and the wanting of a woman and make them his own.

*1860, the Wyoming Territory
at the foot of the Wind River Range,
where the red man's arrows made
no choice between courage and cowardice,
wise men and fools . . .*

1

He listened to the sound in the dawn mists, the faint but unmistakable splashing of water. The big man with the lake-blue eyes rose from his bedroll in the thicket of burr oak and pulled on trousers and gun belt. He had taken note of the pond a few dozen yards along the ridge before he'd settled down to sleep, but he'd seen no one near. The faint splashing sounds came again and he began to move forward in a crouch, the morning mists a frayed white scarf that lay along the ground. On steps silent as a bobcat's tread, he pushed his way through the mists that doggedly clung to the land, climbing the gentle slope that rode to the flat ridge. The sound grew stronger, water rippling, being churned, and the pond came into sight as he dropped to one knee.

He peered through the drifting mists at the water and spied the figure that rose up from below the surface. He saw the swimmer's long, thin arms, a shock of black hair that glistened with wetness. He heard the oath fall from his lips as he watched the figure turn and roll with easy grace in the water.

"I'll be goddammed," he muttered as he stared at the girl. She moved higher out of the water as she turned, enough for him to see the curve of lovely white breasts before they vanished into the pond. The big man moved forward again, with short, darting steps inside the thick underbrush, and as the girl turned on her back, he caught a glimpse of one pink tip that pushed up over the surface of the water.

Skye Fargo moved still closer to the pond as the mists continued to be shredded further by the morning sun. But the dawn mist still clung with enough wispy strength to shroud most of the pond with gray puffballs that rolled not unlike a kind of vaporous tumbleweed. He edged still closer and settled down on one knee in the brush to enjoy the moment of unexpected beauty, even as he wondered where this water nymph had come from in the dawn.

The girl turned again, dived under the surface, and he watched her shiny-wet, beautiful little rear rise up for an instant and then disappear. He decided he could move a few steps closer, and he was almost to the edge of the pond when he froze in place as his nostrils flared and drew in the odor of buckskin loincloths rubbed smooth with fish oil and hair slicked down with bear grease. It was a scent that meant only one thing, and the dawn wind blew it to him from north along the broad, tree-covered rise.

He drew in another deep breath. The scent was stronger. They were heading toward the pond, and from the slightly musky pervasiveness of it he guessed they weren't more than a hundred yards away.

The girl had surfaced again, thoroughly enjoying herself as she played otter in the pond. When the bucks reached the pond, it could well be her last swim. Fargo grimaced and started to rise, but quickly lowered himself again. The Indians were still a few minutes away, but if she screamed, they'd be here instantly and he knew that if he just appeared she could well be startled into a scream.

"Shit," he muttered as the odor of buck grew still stronger. He moved to the edge of the bushes, reached down, and picked up a small stone. If he could turn startle into surprise, he might avoid a scream, he figured. He tossed the stone into the water; it landed only a few inches from her with a soft plunking sound and the girl turned instantly in the water. He stepped from the brush as she stared at the water for a moment, then turned to frown at the shore.

When she saw him, he was in a crouch, one finger held against his lips in the universal gesture of silence. The stone had alerted her to a surprise and his gesture froze her reaction into a tiny gasp. He saw round dark-blue eyes peering back from under the frown, and she sank under the water at once till only her head showed. He slowly drew the finger from his lips and his voice was filled with whispered urgency.

"Don't make a damn sound," he said. "Swim, underwater, to the other side of the pond, to that willow hanging low over the water." She turned as she tread water to peer across the pond. "You can come up for air underneath the branches," he said, and she turned back to him, starting to open her mouth to answer. "Now, dammit," he hissed.

She caught the urgent command in his voice, drew a deep breath, and disappeared under the surface of the pond. He waited, his eyes on the weeping willow across the water. Finally he saw her head bob up, all but invisible in the small space between the long, low-hanging leaves and the water.

The gray-white mists continued to drift along the surface of the pond and he suddenly heard the sound of horses moving slowly through the woods. He backed quickly into a thick clump of buttonbush and peered again across the pond to the willow. Unless they made a deliberate search for her, they'd not spot her under the tree with just a casual scan of the pond.

Satisfied, Fargo began to move back deeper into the buttonbush when his glance froze at the edge of the pond. "Goddamn," he swore as he stared at the small, neat pile of clothes at the edge of the pond, the brown dress, pink bloomers and petticoat atop it, and a towel over all. They see the clothes and then they'd surely scour the pond until they found her.

He cursed again silently as he listened for another moment. Three horses, he guessed, maybe two, he couldn't be certain. But they were a damn-sight closer now. But he had to try to snatch the clothes away. He rose to a crouch and darted from the brush on long-legged, silent strides. His hand had just closed around the garments when he heard the guttural grunt of surprise. He didn't turn to look but flung himself sideways as his ears caught the hiss of an arrow as it was released from its bow. He caught a glimpse of the feathered shaft plunging into the pile of clothes where his hand had been, and he kept rolling. He came up on one knee and started to draw the Colt. But he let it drop back into its holster.

He saw three bucks, naked except for loincloths, but there could be others near. If so, shots would sure as hell bring them on the run. He stayed on one knee as he saw one of the attackers, a lance held upraised, spur his pony forward. Fargo stayed, counted off seconds, his eyes measuring distance, speed, angles. The Indian held the lance in his right hand, and Fargo, his mouth a thin, tight line, dared to stay motionless another few split seconds. With the short-legged pony almost atop him, he gathered the steel-spring muscles in his legs and leapt to his right. The attacking brave had to make a quick change, crossing his arm in front of him to fling the lance. It was enough to shatter his rhythm and his aim, and the lance went wide, embedding itself in the soft earth of the shoreline.

As the Indian yanked hard on the pony to rein up, Fargo spun and yanked the lance from the earth. He flung it with all his strength at the man directly in front of him and saw the lance hurtle into the Indian's abdomen. Fargo dropped to all fours and spun as two arrows whistled past his head while his victim pitched forward from his horse, both hands helplessly clutching at the lance that had come out his back.

Fargo half-ran, half-dived into the pond as another arrow whistled over his head. He went down underwater instantly, and swam halfway down along one side of the pond, staying far away from the willow tree. The two braves would be searching the water, waiting for him to surface, and he did so when he was but a few feet from the shoreline halfway down the side of the pond. They spotted him at once and started to race their ponies toward him. But Fargo struck for the shore, pressed feet into soft muddy earth, and raced out of the water and into the heavy woods. He glanced to his left to see the nearest buck let another arrow fly and then rein his pony up as he leapt to the ground.

Fargo dropped to one knee and yanked the double-edged throwing knife from its calf holster around his leg. He saw the Indian, an arrow poised on his bowstring, start to move carefully through the woods. The sun had come up to flood the forest with light, and Fargo raised his arm, the perfectly balanced, thin blade poised to throw. He stayed motionless, not even drawing a breath, watching the man pass a tree, come into full view. With a snap of his wrist, Fargo flung the blade and saw it slam into the buck's throat just above his collarbone. The Indian staggered in a half-circle, the bow and arrow falling from his hands, and he finally collapsed as he futilely pawed at the thin blade that protruded from the base of his throat.

Fargo half-rose as the third brave, also on foot now, came toward him, a jagged-edged bone-scraping knife in one hand. The buck, tall with a thin, narrow face and slitted eyes, moved with quick grace through the woods, his long body naked except for a loincloth. He held the bone-scraping knife in his right hand, raised to lash out in any direction. Fargo forced himself to keep from drawing the big Colt at his side as he moved to one side, then the other. But the Indian's long form swayed to match his every move.

Fargo took a hard step forward, darted sideways, and spotted a small glen in the forest. He moved into it, the Indian coming after him on quick, lithe steps. The buck made a feint with the knife and Fargo reacted, pulled away, and felt the blade graze his arm. The Indian had plainly planned for his move.

The buck came in again, trying another feint, but this time Fargo only backed away and his foe grunted in disappointment. But he advanced once more, swinging the jagged bone blade in a half-circle. Fargo halted suddenly, tried a long left jab, and the Indian swept the blade upward instantly. The Trailsman felt it graze his forearm as he drew back. But he jabbed again with his left and again the buck swept the blade upward. Fargo feinted a jab and saw the jagged knife start to sweep up but halt as the Indian pulled back. Fargo's inward smile was a grimace, but he had learned one thing: the brave's reactions could be predicted. To be certain, he danced forward on the balls of his feet and tried a lunge to take hold of the brave's wrist. The buck dropped into a half-crouch and lashed out with the knife in a flat arc that made Fargo suck his stomach in as he fell back. He'd tried a different attack and received a different counteraction. He moved back again, letting the brave come toward him.

His every muscle ready, Fargo lashed out with another jab and the Indian again swept his bone knife upward, but this time the Trailsman didn't pull the jab back. Instead, he dropped his arm, brought it up sharply, his hand closing around the Indian's elbow. He pushed up, twisted, and the man spun around off-balance. Fargo's right came around with all his strength to smash into the buck's spine. He heard the shattering of bone and the Indian gave a wild cry of pain as he fell forward. He was on his knees on the ground, still groaning as Fargo's kick smashed into the exact same spot in his spine.

With a terrible cry of pain, the man pitched forward and lay facedown in the grass, his body quivering almost convulsively until finally his hands grew stiff, becoming clawlike for an instant before he lay still. Fargo backed away, strode to the nearest still form, and retrieved the thin-bladed throwing knife, wiped it clean on the grass, and returned it to its calf holster.

He moved from the foliage to the edge of the pond. The last threads of the dawn mist were drifting away and he waved to the distant head still under the arch of the willow. He saw the young woman begin to swim toward him and he dropped to one knee as he waited. She neared, making certain that only her head and shoulders were visible as she halted and tread water.

He frowned at her. "Get the hell out of there before we have more company," he rasped.

"I'm not getting out with you standing there," she said.

"Damn, I'll never understand women," Fargo muttered. "You're more worried over your modesty than your scalp."

"No, I'm just not putting on an exhibition," she said.

"I'll go get my horse. If you're not toweled dry and dressed by the time I get back, I'll help you," Fargo said. He turned on his heel and strode into the woods. He walked back to where he'd bedded down, finished dressing, and saddled the Ovaro and led the horse back to the pond.

The girl was dressed in a brown dress fitted at the waist that fell over what seemed a nice shape with very high, very round breasts. He took in the still-glistening wet black hair that fell shoulder-length, deep-blue eyes, a straight nose, and well-formed pale-red lips, a face that held a certain feistiness that added a spirit to what would otherwise have been merely attractive.

"You want to tell me where you came from and why you were paddling around in this pond at dawn?" Fargo asked, disapproval in his voice.

"I came from the wagons camped down below the ridge. I saw this pond yesterday when I rode up this way," she answered. "I woke early and decided to come up for a bath and a swim."

"Don't you know the kind of country this is, honey?" Fargo frowned.

"Of course I know it's wild and dangerous, if that's what you mean."

"That's what I mean," he grunted.

"I didn't think they'd be riding about this early."

"Deer hunting is good in the early dawn," Fargo said. "You've a name?"

"Trudy Deakens," the girl said, and her eyes went to the buck with the lance sticking from him and Fargo saw her shudder. The buck wore a wrist gauntlet and he peered at the markings on it.

"Arapaho," he said. "This is pretty much at the end of Arapaho country. You're lucky. They were probably just a stray band out hunting."

Trudy Deakens returned her eyes to him. "I never heard them."

"Indians don't go around making much noise," Fargo said blandly.

"But you heard them," she said.

"Educated ears." He saw the frost come into her eyes.

"You want to tell me how long you were watching before they came?" she queried.

"You mean how much did I see?" He grinned and her frosty silence answered. "Just enough to want to see more," he said, and saw the touch of color come into her cheeks.

"I never thought I'd be grateful to a Peeping Tom," Trudy said.

"I guess you'll have to change your mind about Peeping Toms," Fargo commented.

"Hardly," she said frostily. "But I am very grateful," she went on, the ice vanishing from her voice. "My uncle's wagon master of the wagons I'm with. We came up two men short. I'm sure he'd be happy to give you a job riding guard for us."

"Got a job."

"Doing what? Riding the woods?"

"I'm on my way to it," Fargo answered calmly.

A moment of disappointment touched her face. "Well, if you change your mind, I know Uncle will be glad to have you," she said, and walked toward a medium-brown horse all but hidden in the trees. He watched as she pulled herself onto the horse and sent the animal forward, and he immediately noticed the limp in the horse's left leg. "I know," she said, reading his eyes. "He pulled a muscle in his foreshoulder."

"Only thing that'll help that is a long rest," Fargo said.

"I know," Trudy said again. "I'll give him to somebody with a ranch where he can rest, and he'll be good as new. Meanwhile, I'll buy a new mount as soon as I can."

Fargo swung onto the Ovaro and saw the girl take in

the beauty of the jet-black fore and hind quarters and the gleaming white midsection.

"That's something special," she said admiringly.

"And not for sale," Fargo returned.

"I'm sure of that," Trudy answered.

Fargo pulled in beside her as she started slowly down the slope from the broad ridge. He reined up halfway down where the wagons came into view below. Three old Conestogas, he saw, and his mouth tightened.

Trudy's remark took him by surprise. "You disapprove," she said.

He turned his lake-blue eyes on her. "You're damn sharp." He smiled.

"It was in your face."

"Most wouldn't have picked up on it," Fargo said.

She shrugged away the compliment. "Why?"

Fargo returned his gaze to the wagons below. "Not small enough and not big enough," he answered, and her eyes waited for him to go on. "One wagon might sneak through. A big, strong train would have a chance at defending itself. You're neither. You're three chickens waiting for a hawk to strike."

"We've done quite well so far," she said defensively.

"Luck. And you haven't gone into real mean Indian country yet," Fargo said. "You seem to be heading west. That means you're going straight into Cheyenne country, with some Shoshoni, Bannock, and Sioux thrown in."

"We'll be joining up with more wagons in a few days," she said.

"I hope so," he told her, and she gave his handsomely chiseled face a long appraisal.

"Now what are you thinking?" she asked.

"I'm thinking this is no country for greenhorns," he said, and saw her dark-blue eyes flare.

"What makes you think we're greenhorns?" She frowned.

"Three wagons, paddling in ponds by yourself, two men short," he snapped.

"Then come join us. Uncle Ben will pay real well."

"I told you I have a job waiting."

"I'm not sure I believe that," Trudy Deakens sniffed.

"Believe whatever you like, honey," Fargo tossed back.

"If you think we're greenhorns in danger, it seems to me you'd have a sense of responsibility to help us."

"I saved your little ass. That's enough responsibility for me."

The touch of anger left her face. "Yes, and I'm grateful to you for that," she said. "I've no right asking more of you."

"You've a right to ask and I've a right to say no," he told her, and she accepted his words with a shrug that said she conceded only half of what he'd said. "You'd best see to that horse of yours."

"At the next town, wherever that is," she said.

"Keep going northwest," he told her. "You'll come to Beaver Falls. You ought to be able to pick up a new mount there."

"I'll tell Uncle Ben," she said. "Is that where you're going?"

He smiled. She was sharp and tenacious and quick. She didn't miss an opportunity and he liked the spirit of her. "Wasn't planning to," he answered.

"That job will be there if you change your mind," she said.

"I won't be doing that."

"No more playing Peeping Tom, either, I trust."

"I didn't say that." Fargo grinned.

She allowed a wry smile to touch her nicely shaped lips. He let his eyes take in the very round, very high breasts that pressed the brown dress outward with not even the mark of a tiny point showing, her legs as she sat the saddle outlined against the dress in lovely, long curves.

"Good luck, Trudy," Fargo said as he started to turn the Ovaro.

"Wait," she called. "You never told me your name."

"Sir Galahad, Peeping Tom, Passer-by, take your pick." He laughed and spurred the pinto up the slope and into the trees.

He stopped in the thick foliage and watched Trudy Deakens continue on down the slope to the three wagons. She'd almost been carried off by three Arapaho bucks. Even though he'd saved her, the specter of it would have reduced most women to distraught shock. But she'd taken it in stride. That feistiness he'd seen in her face ran deep. She'd need every bit of toughness she had before her journey was over, he was certain.

He watched her reach the three wagons, dismount, and turn to peer up into the hills where she'd left him. He sent the pinto forward through the hills and knew a furrow had dug into his brow. He wondered why he had the feeling he hadn't seen the last of Trudy Deakens.

2

Fargo rode unhurriedly and turned into the cool of the woods. He wasn't expected in Crooked Branch till the week's end and he'd planned on enjoying a relaxed and leisurely journey, as much as that was possible in a land where death could come suddenly in a dozen different ways. He stayed in the woodland that ran almost parallel to the valleylike, long lowland beneath, and he spotted plenty of unshod Indian pony prints, none terribly new. He enjoyed the dense clusters of orange milkweed, which set the forest afire, and the greenish yellow of Indian cucumber, which offered a cool, soothing vista. When morning neared an end, he found a glen surrounded by the filmy delicacy of Queen Anne's lace and he halted to stretch out on a bed of elf-cup moss.

He dozed, woke, dozed again, and dimly listened to the sounds of the yellow warbler and the softer coo of the mourning dove and leisurely returned to the saddle when the afternoon wore on. He followed the slow curve of the woodland, and the trees spread out to let him see down into the lower terrain. He reined to a halt. An almost straight ribbon of green-blue, calm water moved from north to south below him, the Hades River, a lone tributary of the Sweetwater that had been carved through the land by a mudslide ages ago.

Something else moved below him, too, three Conestogas that rolled toward the river, and Fargo's lips pulled back in a grimace: the Hades was a river of deception that had lured many an unwary traveler to disaster. A figure in a brown dress rode a half-dozen yards ahead of the Conestogas.

Trudy's lame horse had been tethered to the back of the last wagon and she rode another mount. Fargo watched her halt at the bank, survey the river, and wave the wagons forward.

"Damn the girl," Fargo murmured aloud. "Damn all greenhorns." He spurred the Ovaro down the slope, reached the bank, and went into a canter that let him reach the riverbank just as the wagons rolled to a halt. He saw the surprise in Trudy Deakens' eyes as he rode up.

"Well, this is a surprise," she said, and glanced at a man who swung down from the lead Conestoga. "This is the man I told you about, Uncle Ben," she said.

"Ben Deakens," the man said as he strode over to Fargo, who took in a smallish man with thinning gray-brown hair and a lined, tired face with eyes that carried a lifetime of small defeats in their pale-blue orbs. "I'm beholden to you, mister," Ben said warmly. "You saved Trudy's life, she tells me."

"Glad I was on hand," Fargo said. "This seems like my day for good deeds."

The man's eyes narrowed a fraction. "Meaning what, exactly?" he asked.

"You can't cross the Hades here," Fargo said.

"Why not?" Trudy cut in. "I've never seen a calmer river. I can see it's not real deep, either."

"Rivers are like women. They can fool you real easy." Fargo smiled.

"Where can we cross?" Ben asked.

"Only safe place is way down where the river bends back and forth. It's near a day's ride," Fargo said.

Trudy's voice cut in. "That'll cost us another day, maybe two. We can't do that."

Fargo saw the hesitation in Ben Deakens' tired eyes. "Guess you'll have to choose between your wagons or your timetable," he said.

The indecision stayed in the man's eyes, but Fargo watched Trudy take command with a quick glance at him and then focusing on her uncle. "Ben, I must tell you that this man, while he did a brave and wonderful thing for me, thinks we've no business here," she said with an edge of disdain in her voice. "In his own way, he thinks he's doing us a favor if he keeps us from going on," she added, and turned a faintly chiding smile at Fargo.

Fargo let a wry smile answer. "You're half-right, honey," he said. "That is what I think, but that's not what I'm doing. I'm just giving you some advice. You can't cross the Hades until way south."

"Nonsense, and I'll prove it," Trudy snapped. Instantly she wheeled her horse and rode into the river.

Fargo saw the apprehension in Ben Deakens' eyes as he watched her. She was touching bottom as she approached midriver, and the Trailsman saw the horse lose contact with its footing and begin to swim. He waited, his lips a thin line. When she had just passed midriver, her horse suddenly half-turned and began to be swept downstream, as Fargo knew it would. He saw Trudy realize she was suddenly in trouble and watched her initial surprise give way to her natural ability to handle a horse. She got the animal's head around, but the current swung it over in the other direction and she had to fight to bring its head around again. Finally she got its rear turned enough so that it faced the current and was able to swim forward. But she was a good fifty yards downriver by then and he watched the horse labor to swim forward at an angle until it was out of the sudden rush of current.

He waited till she reached the shore and slowly rode back.

There was a hint of triumph in her eyes. "It's a sudden and strong current in midriver. It takes you by surprise," she said. "But you knew about it, didn't you?" He nodded and said nothing. "It can be handled. It's not that deep out there. The wagons will still be touching bottom. We'll make it across."

"You won't," Fargo said.

"I know about the current now. We'll prepare for it. We can handle it," Trudy said adamantly.

Fargo felt Ben's eyes search his face for a concession. He found none and the man turned to Trudy as she broke into his thoughts.

"It's quite plain that we can cross. I proved it," she said. "Fargo just doesn't want to admit it. He still wants us to get discouraged and turn back."

Fargo remained silent as he debated with himself and he swept the other two wagons with a slow survey. He took in two families in one, three in another, all earnest, all youthful, and all full of hope with more than enough kids looking on in wide-eyed excitement. He decided against saying anything further. He'd be doing them a favor by letting them end their trek right here.

"I've said my piece," he remarked, deciding to offer no more than that.

" 'Fraid I'll have to go along with Trudy, taking in what she showed us," Ben Deakens said with an apologetic shrug. The man was wagon master but the real strength lay with his niece, Fargo decided. He tipped his hat and moved his horse backward. Deakens climbed onto the lead Conestoga and waved the others forward while Trudy came over to where the man with the lake-blue eyes watched impassively.

"I know you tried to do what you think is right," she said.

He smiled at the condescension in her voice and knew she didn't catch the ice under the smile. "Guess so," he said.

Trudy turned her horse and moved into the river a few paces ahead of the Conestoga with her uncle at the reins. Fargo watched the other wagons roll into the river, the water rising along their sides as they rolled down the gently sloping bottom. Trudy's horse lost contact with the bottom as she neared midriver, and began to swim again. She half-circled the mount so it'd move forward into the sudden current. She was smart, a quick learn, he admitted with a trace of grudgingness. His eyes went to the Conestogas. While their teams began to swim, the heavy wagons stayed touching the bottom.

Fargo grimaced inwardly. The current was a freak, a high-speed stream that coursed down the center of the river where the bottom formed a sudden trench. The straightness of the river let it race along gathering speed with every mile. But it wasn't the current that was going to do them in, not by itself. It was the river bottom along the edge of the trench, its own combination of silt, mud, and fine sand that formed a sucking ooze. The horses would swim over it but the loaded wagons would stay on the bottom, wheels gripped and held fast as though they'd been shackled. As he watched, the water began to slide along the lower edges of their canvas tops and Deakens' Conestoga reached midriver with a second wagon close behind it.

Fargo saw them come to a sudden halt while, at the same instant, they came into the swift current. The waters pulled hard at the horses suddenly unable to swim forward as the mired wagons held them back. The animals began to panic almost at once as they were pulled sideways against shafts. Trying to swim, caught by the current and the immovable wagons, Ben Deakens' team half-rose in the water, smashed sideways, and Fargo saw the wagon begin to tilt on one side. A quick glance showed the second Conestoga was in trouble, too, its team also being pulled sideways by the current. It would be only moments before it, too, began to tilt over. Fargo sent the Ovaro splashing into the river.

"Unhitch the teams," he shouted. "Cut the harneses before they take you over." He glimpsed Trudy riding to her uncle's aid while two men in the second wagon leapt from the driver's seat and one, with a small hand ax, began to sever the traces and the breechings as the other released the reins.

Deakens' wagon was beginning to tip badly and Fargo rode toward it as he yanked the double-edged blade from his calf holster. He reached the horses, saw Trudy pulling the reins free, and he began to sever the bellyband and yank the breeching loose. The panicked horses did the rest as they pulled forward, flailing the water with their powerful bodies. This last, wrenching pull slammed into the shaft and Fargo yanked the Ovaro backward as the Conestoga went over. He saw Ben Deakens leap clear of the wagon and hit the water. Forward of the wagon, Trudy swam her horse out of danger. Fargo brought his own mount onto firmer ground and saw that the second Conestoga had avoided going over and the third one had reined up before hitting midriver.

Ben Deakens swam for shore while Trudy grasped the cheek straps of the team that now swam freely, and began to bring the horses around.

Fargo rode to where the second Conestoga stayed rooted in the silt and mud while the water swirled more than halfway up the side of the canvas top. Two youngsters peered out from the front of the wagon while two women and two more youngsters leaned from the tailgate.

"Pass me the kids, two for a start," Fargo called as he brought the pinto alongside, the horse swimming hard against the pushing, dragging power of the current. He reached out, gathered in first one, then the other child, and held them in the saddle in front of him as he rode back to shore. The youngsters dropped down before he was fully back on dry ground and he returned to the Conestoga, where he took the other two youngsters.

"We'll swim back," one of the men called out, and Fargo saw him go into the water with a woman clinging to his arm. The current immediately swept them downriver until they had a chance to swim their way out of it. By now Fargo had deposited the other two kids on the riverbank. Trudy, leading the team, reached the bank and passed him and avoided his eyes.

Ben Deakens, gathering his breath on one knee, stared at the other couples as they trudged their way from the water. "Nobody hurt, thank God," he murmured, and rose to face the big man on the Ovaro and there was more defeat than bitterness in his eyes. "Seems you were right, mister," he admitted.

"A hard-swimming horse can get through the center current, even being swept downriver some," Fargo said. "But the bottom's too soft to support wagons. It sucked them in while the current pulled at the horses who weren't touching bottom, sort of like a fighter holding a man in place with one hand and hitting him with the other."

"How'd you know that?" Ben asked.

"Been over it before. Saw too many who didn't make it. That's why it's called the Hades. It's calm on top and hell underneath."

One of the other men spoke, his wife and children clinging to him. "We just stand by and watch our wagons break up?"

"No, you can get them out if you do it right and get at it right away," Fargo said.

"How?"

"You've six strong horses. On land, hitched together, they can pull the wagons free of that ooze," Fargo said. "Get every piece of rope you have."

As the others hurried to the third Conestoga, Fargo saw Trudy's eyes regarding him with a strange mixture of warmth and coolness, gratitude and hostility. He took his eyes from her as a man came up on one of the extra horses with his arms full of good strong hemp.

"I'm Cy Estes from the third wagon along with the Wilsons and the Reicherts. How can we help?" he asked.

"You and the other two men ride out with me and help tie these ropes onto the wagon still standing," Fargo said.

The man nodded and handed him one of the coils of rope.

Fargo immediately started into the river. The three men caught up to him as he neared the Conestoga and he gestured to the wagon. "Tie them tight from the frame of the body," Fargo said, and began to secure one end of the coil of rope he carried. He called back to the others on the shore as he looped the rope under the tailgate. "Hitch the horses together," he ordered, and Ben Deakens quickly moved the others into action.

Fargo returned his attention to the wagon as he kept the Ovaro paddling upriver against the current. With difficulty, the swift current turning their horses too often, the other men managed to get their ropes secured to the big wagon, and when they finished, Fargo motioned them back to the shore.

Stretching the rope he held in one hand, he reached shore and handed the hemp to Deakens. "Hitch it to the horses. Loop it around their chests so it takes the full pull," he said, and waited till the task was finished and five lengths of rope stretched to the Conestoga in midriver. "Move the horses into the water but close to the shore," he ordered, and rode to the front of the first of the three teams. He led the horses forward until the ropes were stretched as taut as possible. "Start them pulling," he shouted, and with the crack of a whip, Ben Deakens moved the horses forward in unison.

Fargo watched the Conestoga shudder and strain and stay fast. "Again, harder," he shouted, and the six horses strained forward. Again, the Conestoga shuddered and still stayed mired fast. The Trailsman felt the apprehension stab at him. He had seen wagons pulled apart, frames cracking open, and these Conestogas were worn specimens, he had long ago noted. His lips pulled back, he shouted at Ben Deakens again and the man snapped his whip hard and the six horses surged forward. His eyes fixed on the wagon, Fargo saw the Conestoga quiver as the crack of the whip resounded again and, with shuddering slowness, the wheels moved. The wagon began to roll from midriver and the swirling current as the sucking ooze reluctantly released its grip.

"Keep 'em going," Fargo shouted as the big wagon continued to move, rolling onto firmer bottom land. Suddenly it began to move almost freely. It rolled at an angle toward the shore, the six horses pulling with ease now. When the wagon rolled onto the dry bank, men and women rushed forward to bring it to a halt, and someone leapt aboard and put on the handbrake.

The horses were brought to a stop and Fargo turned to stare across the water on at Conestoga on its side in midriver. One of the other men came up and introduced himself as Jay Wilson. "We just leave that one?" he asked.

"No, we try to get it out," Fargo answered as he started to nose the Ovaro back into the river. "Bring all the ropes," he called to Wilson. He was just short of midriver, surveying the Conestoga, when the others reached him. "We pull it upright first," he said. "Attach your ropes only to the right side of the frame." He supervised the others as they secured their ropes only to the one side of the wagon as he'd directed. "Take them back to the horses," he said as he stayed in the river near the big wagon.

Ben Deakens snapped the whip over the three teams as soon as the ropes were in place and Fargo watched as the Conestoga righted itself more easily than he had expected. He called the teams to a halt while two more ropes were attached to the other side of the wagon. The left wheels seemed to be unbroken, Fargo saw from a cursory inspection, and he credited the cushioning of the water and the mud for that. Once again he motioned to the shore and Ben Deakens put the six horses into motion again. After a wavering start, the Conestoga rolled smoothly enough and was finally pulled onto the riverbank.

Fargo followed and dismounted as Deakens crawled beneath the wagon to inspect the undercarriage. "Nothing broken," he said, his voice heavy with relief. "Hubcaps are loosened but we can tighten them." He crawled from under the wagon and stood up to scan the Conestoga. " 'Course, we'll have to take the canvas down and dry out everything inside." He turned to Fargo as the others quickly gathered around. "I'm beholden to you, again, mister," Deakens said.

"We're all beholden to you," Cy Estes added. "And we don't even know your name."

"Name's Fargo . . . Skye Fargo," the big man said.

"We'd pay top dollar if you'd put in with us, Fargo," Ben Deakens said.

"He has a job, or so he says," Trudy cut in coolly.

"So he says, and so he does." Fargo smiled at her.

"We'll be taking your advice this time," Deakens said. "We'll go south till dark, then camp and go on to that crossing place, come morning. Where the river bends back and forth, you said."

"That's right. It breaks the midriver current up," Fargo said.

"We'd be obliged if you'd ride along and take supper with us," Deakens said.

"Thanks but I'll be riding on." Fargo smiled.

One of the other men stepped forward to offer his hand. "Bill Wilson," he said. "We're all mighty grateful." His handshake was followed by the others, wives included. Only when they began to return to their wagons did Trudy come forward, her eyes studying him with cool appraisal.

"Being grateful comes hard to you, doesn't it?" Fargo speared.

"No. I'm very grateful. I just see more than the others," she returned.

"Such as?"

"I'm trying to read you. You told us not to cross and I didn't listen to you. But you could've spelled it out more," Trudy accused.

"Would you have listened more?" He smiled again.

"Maybe," she said crossly.

"Like hell, and you know it, honey," he snapped, and her half-shrug was an admission.

"But you didn't try," she said. "That's what's important, you didn't try. You sat back to watch us do ourselves in. Then your conscience got the better of you and you helped save things for us."

He laughed. She was both accurate and astute, he realized again. "You make up a good story, I'll say that," he answered, unwilling to give her more.

"I'm right," Trudy said smugly. "And you don't want to ride along because you think we'll get into more trouble."

"With you along, I'm sure of it," he speared, and her eyes shot deep-blue sparks.

"That's a rotten thing to say. You need lessons in manners."

"You need lessons in listening," he answered calmly.

She glared at him, the very high, very round breasts pressed tight against the brown dress with still not the slightest sign of a tiny tip.

He swung onto the Ovaro and felt her eyes on him as he turned the horse.

"I'm not a bad omen," she called out, hurt as well as anger in her voice.

"No, you're not." He laughed as he spurred the Ovaro forward. "Just a pain in the ass."

She called something back but he didn't catch the words as he sent the horse into the river in a spray-splashing gallop. When the horse lost touch with the bottom, he was still galloping and fell into a strong paddling swim that carried him right through the swift midriver current and out onto the other side only a few yards downriver. Fargo turned, waved to Trudy Deakens, who was still standing on the opposite bank as he rode onto the shore and turned south in the approaching dusk.

He rode on unhurriedly as Trudy lingered in his thoughts. He'd told himself he hadn't seen the last of her after their first meeting, and he'd been right. Twice was enough, pretty as she was. She spelled trouble and he put her behind him as he rode on. He could only hope that she'd be lucky. This was a wild and savage land beyond that gave no concession to high-spirited prettiness and laughed at fools and dreamers.

Night slid across the land, a soft black blanket. Fargo found a hollow to bed down and he let sleep take command of the world.

3

Morning came in on warm winds. He rose and found a stream where he washed, filled his canteen, and watered the Ovaro. As a matter of habit, he picked up the horse's left forefoot, examined the shoe, and went on to the right forefoot. A tiny furrow creased his brow, and by the time he'd examined all four of the horse's feet, the crease had become a furrow. The shoes were all worn, much more than he liked to see, and a horse with worn shoes was a horse headed for trouble, he knew. He'd have to make a stop at Beaver Falls. There was a blacksmith there but . . . His lips pulled back in a grimace. He'd intended to avoid Beaver Falls on the way north. Ellie Schneider still lived there, he felt sure, and he remembered how they had parted two years ago. He'd also told Trudy Deakens to go there to find herself a new mount.

Damn, he swore even as he realized he'd no choice. He had to go there to have the pinto reshod. But there was a good chance he could go in and out without seeing Ellie or Trudy. He'd reach the town before the Conestogas arrived and he'd just keep a sharp eye out for Ellie. A wry smile touched his lips as he pulled himself onto the horse. It would be good to see Ellie Schneider again, if he could wipe away their last time together. She'd wanted him to stay and he knew that was impossible. Maybe he hadn't handled it the best way, but it had seemed that to him at the time. It still

34

did, but he was pretty damn sure Ellie'd not agree. He'd stay out of her sight. That was still the wisest thing, he decided, and he rode across low hills, lush with box elder, red cedar, staghorn sumac, and Rocky Mountain maple.

He rode slowly, aware that he'd still arrive in Crooked Branch with plenty of time to spare, even with the delay, and his thoughts drifted to the letter in his saddlebag that had brought him here. The bank check for two hundred dollars had come with it, the kind of advance money no one would turn down. The letter had reached him care of General Delivery back in South Dakota, and he reread it in his mind as he rode, again impressed by the authority and brevity of it.

I'm going to need the very best and I'm told that's you, Fargo. Ed Berrigan said so, as did Homer Stiles. Check with both if you like. I'll want you to take a wagon train for me. Four hundred dollars, two hundred here with this letter. Leave word for me at the mail depot in Arkville. If it's yes, meet me in Crooked Branch, Wyoming Territory July 26.

Oliver Kragg

The letter dropped from his mind and Fargo thought again about what had been left unsaid . . . Trouble. Danger. Problems. Those words were in there between the lines. No one offered the kind of money for a rocking-chair ride. But he'd never turned down top money because it meant trouble, and there was no point in starting now. He'd left his acceptance at the Arkville Mail depot and gone on to finish a job for Sam Jenkins, and now he was riding the warm countryside of the Wyoming Territory. And he was seeing enough Indian pony prints to make him more cautious than usual as he nosed the Ovaro slowly through and around clusters of shadbush.

The afternoon had worn down when he reached Beaver Falls and rode slowly through the bustling town. It drew mostly east-west travelers, the only town due west of the North Platte. He rode with his eyes moving over the cowhands and drifters, the miners with their pack mules and Owensboro seed-bed wagons, searching the bustling main street for sight of a smallish figure with light-brown hair pulled high atop her head, a short nose, round cheeks, and a quick, determined stride. But no one fit the description and he kept moving on down the street, past the saloon, and halted a dozen yards on at the blacksmith's shop. Just back of the smithy, a horse trader had two long corrals with a dozen horses inside them and a sign on the fencepost that read: MALACHY'S—GOOD HORSES—GOOD PRICES.

Fargo's practiced eye swept the mounts in the corral. A few were good, the rest were a lot less than good. He turned his attention to the young boy who emerged from the blacksmith shop. "Smithy had to go out of town on a job," the boy said. "He'll be back in the shop first thing in the morning."

"Damn the luck," Fargo swore, and knew he had no choice but to wait for morning. There was no other town within a hundred miles. He dismounted and led the horse back down main street, past the saloon, still watching for a familiar face and figure. He halted when he spied a man selling buffalo sandwiches from a narrow storefront. They smelled good and looked good. He tethered the Ovaro, stepped into the tiny store, and ordered one of the sandwiches replete with onion, pickle, and lemon juice.

He found he was hungrier than he'd realized, and ate the sandwich with gusto, washed it down with a mug of tap beer. When he finished, he stepped back into the street and scanned the scene again and began to retrace steps out of town. Ellie had her own seamstress shop at the other end of town, and he'd go no closer to it than the smithy, he promised himself. He'd gone perhaps another hundred feet down the street, the Ovaro walking behind him, when he came to a halt. "Stop right there, Skye Fargo," the voice said, crisp, commanding and familiar.

"Damn," he muttered, and slowly turned to see the smallish figure striding toward him, tightly curled light-brown hair tossing, a nicely balanced figure that made her seem more voluptuous than she actually was.

"You really thought you could get away with it?" the young woman snapped.

"Get away with what?" Fargo asked innocently.

"Sneaking through town with a horse even a blind man would stop to look at."

"I wasn't sneaking through town. I was going to come visit." Fargo told himself it wasn't a real lie, more of a possibility still undecided. "You look right fine, Ellie," he said, the words more than an attempt to defuse her anger. She did indeed look well, her small face still pretty, blue eyes bright, cheeks still full and nicely rounded. Her light-blue blouse pressed forward with undeniable attractiveness and her hips were still slender.

"What are you doing here, Fargo?" Ellie Schneider asked firmly.

"Passing through. Stopped at the smithy, but he won't be back till morning," Fargo said. The young woman's face stayed set and unsmiling. "You doing well, Ellie?" he asked.

"Well enough," Ellie snapped back. "There are things I've been saving to say."

"Two years of letting things churn inside you? That's

not good for you," he said, and tried to be more concerned than chiding.

"You're a fine one to talk about what's good for me," the young woman flung back. "You just follow along with me." She spun on her heel, crossed the street, and stepped into a pony cart.

Fargo led the Ovaro along behind him as he fell in step behind the cart that Ellie drove down the street. She halted in front of the house at the other end of town and Fargo felt the rush of familiarity sweep through him. When he followed her into the house, he saw that she had redone the front room with bright, flowered wallpaper that gave the house a becoming airiness.

"Real nice," he commented as he faced her stern, set countenance. "Why don't we talk about now, not yesterday?" he suggested with a smile.

Her eyes failed to soften even a fraction. "I deserved better then. I deserve an explanation now," Ellie Schneider bit out. "I never figured you for one who'd go sneaking away in the night like a thief."

"You put it hard."

"Is there another way?"

"Different words can put a different face on it."

"What different words?" Ellie demanded.

"It's sometimes kinder to be cruel."

"Is that what you were doing, being kind?"

"Yes, if you want the truth. I told you I wasn't going to stay, I'd things unfinished to do and you wouldn't listen," he told her. "I finished helping your pa and your brothers and I had to move on."

"And I wanted you to come back with me and talk it out," Ellie said.

"Talk it out in bed and everywhere else." Fargo smiled. "There'd have been tears and wailing and all kinds of upset for you. The pain would've only been dragged out. My way was quick and it left you with all your anger."

"Was that supposed to help?"

"Anger always helps the hurting," he said gently, and saw the deep sigh that drew her shoulders and breasts upward.

"I guess it did. It gave me something to hold on to besides the hurt. I did hate you, Skye Fargo. I hated you with every part of me."

"And you'd really no cause, Ellie. I always told you I'd not be staying."

Ellie's voice grew soft, filled with bittersweet rememberings. "Yes, you did, and you're right, I wouldn't listen. I remember all of it, the good and the bad."

"Mostly it was good," Fargo said, and she nodded and sank into the small settee behind her.

"Come sit down," she said. "It's suddenly all unimportant now. I've waited so long to face you and now it doesn't mean all that much. I feel better, though, like finally being able to close a door."

He folded himself beside her and saw her smile, the half-sly, half-quiet smile that had always been a part of her.

"Would you have come visit on your own?" she asked.

"I'd have thought hard about it," he said.

She laughed. "You haven't changed your answers any," Ellie said. "How long are you staying in Beaver Falls?"

"Till tomorrow, when I can get a set of new shoes for the Ovaro."

"I've still an extra room. You're welcome to it," she said, and smiled at the flash of apprehension that touched his face. "No asking you to stay longer, I promise. No more anger or tears. I guess seeing you broke all that up. I've still some of that good bourbon left."

"Now, that sounds like a good idea," Fargo said. He watched her go to a cabinet and bring out glasses and a bottle, moving with the quick, bright steps that had always been hers, her small rear turning, modest breasts swaying gracefully.

She poured the bourbon and raised her glass in a toast. "To all the wonderful things we knew together," she said, and he nodded and took a long draw of the whiskey.

Fargo felt himself relaxing and they talked about past times with the special warmth that comes of looking back. At her prodding, he told her of some of the trails he'd taken since that time, and night came to embrace the house. Ellie put a lamp on low and insisted on fixing a supper of leftovers.

"What about you, Ellie? Nobody waiting to ride off with you?" he asked.

"There've been a few, but you know I was always particular. And maybe I've been holding on to too many wrong things."

"Maybe it'll be different now," Fargo offered gently, and she nodded and flashed a bright smile.

"Yes, I think it will be. Seeing you, talking to you again, it's sort of like opening a window inside," Ellie said, and she rose, came to him, and put both hands against his face. "I'll never forget all the good things, Fargo. I'll keep thinking about them from now on." She stepped back, pulled him to his feet. "And the room's still yours. We're only old friends now, Fargo."

"All right. A real bed sounds inviting," he said, and she gestured to the room.

"Good night," Ellie said, and she turned away.

" 'Night," he returned, and went into the small extra room. The lone window let in the moonlight and he didn't bother with the lamp as he undressed and stretched out naked on the bed. He felt good. It had all gone well, Ellie's fury something she'd clung to out of the past and now put into proper place. He frowned at himself as he toyed with idle thoughts he'd no right to toy with. He was pushing them from his mind when he heard the faint click of the door latch and the door opened.

Ellie came into the room, a filmy, short nightgown clinging to her body. "I know what you were thinking," she murmured.

"You do? How?" Fargo asked as he pushed himself onto his elbows.

"Because I was thinking the same thing. You were thinking it'd be nice to turn the clock back," she said, and he had no need to answer as she came to him, flung the wispy nightgown off, and brought her soft, slender nakedness against him. Her lips closed over his as she pressed down over him, sweet, curving breasts flattening against his chest, tiny brown-pink tips little points that almost tickled. Ellie's arms went around his neck and her lips worked, sucked, pressed, her tongue sliding, darting, offering, and he felt her slender body quivering against him.

"Oh, God, Fargo, so long to wait, so long to want," she murmured, and her legs rose, climbed up along his body as he felt himself responding to her, his strength swelling at once to press against the small, curly-wire triangle that was Ellie's. "Yes, yes, oh, yes, Fargo . . . oh, oh," she half-cried, and she was suddenly a quivering, shaking, wanting dervish, exploding with all the pent-up emotions inside her. She drew her knees up and sank down over him, impaling her warm, flowing self over him, plunging deep, drawing up at once and plunging down again as the screams tore from her throat each time. She fell forward over him, brought her breasts to his mouth, where he took in first one, then the other while Ellie continued to plunge down over him.

He felt his own burgeoning strength filling her, pressing against the soft, luscious walls. She cried out again and again at the pleasure of it. The intensity of her was different than anything he remembered, almost a wild anger transformed into furious ecstasy, and when the spiraling climax began inside her, she threw her head back, arching her body as she furiously pumped atop him. Her screams reverberated from wall to wall in the little room. She held, prolonged, her cries faltering as ecstasy slipped away, the world of pure pleasure shattering all too soon, and she fell down across him, her breath coming in low, rasped heaving sounds.

"Oh, my God, oh, God, Fargo . . . oh, oooooh," Ellie gasped as, finally, she straightened her legs and rolled from him with a shuddering gasp. He gazed at her slender shape, which still quivered, the senses unwilling to give up pleasure, and she finally lay still as he folded her into his arms.

"You turn the clock back real well," Ellie murmured.

"You did most of the turning, honey," Fargo said as she clung hard against him.

"The night's young," Ellie murmured, and he felt her hands moving slowly down his hard-packed frame.

"It is," he agreed, and she closed her eyes, slept in his arms until she woke and once again the small room echoed with her cries of pure gratification until her final screams spiraled into the night and she fell hard asleep against him.

He rose when morning came, but Ellie clung to him. "I'll make breakfast," she said. "You've time for that." He nodded agreement, and after he'd washed and dressed, he enjoyed the slender sweetness of her as, still in the filmy nightgown, she made coffee and biscuits.

"You're not using words," he told her when he finished the coffee. "That's the only difference."

She paused, her smile one of sheepish admittance. "Old yearnings die hard," she said, and brushed his cheek with her lips as he rose to leave. "Come back and stay here if you have to wait. I won't be here. I have to do a fitting at Emma McKenzie's."

He waved back at her as she watched him from the doorway.

He led the Ovaro down the main street of the town. The smith was already at work when he reached the shop. The man gave the horse a glance of quick admiration and examined his hooves. "Got a few waiting ahead of you since yesterday," the blacksmith said. "Leave him and come back early afternoon."

"Obliged," Fargo said, and strolled away to pause at the horse dealer's corrals back of the blacksmith's shop. Again, his eye picked out only two or three good, sound animals as he watched the man feed his stock.

"Looking for a horse, mister?" the man asked.

"No, just looking," Fargo said.

"When you do, remember Malachy," the man said. "I'm the only horse dealer in town."

"I'll do that," Fargo said, and walked on his way. He sauntered through the town and then, remembering that Trudy could arrive at any time with the Conestogas, he hurried back to Ellie's place. He made himself another cup of coffee and relaxed in an easy chair and listened to the sounds of the town outside. He dozed, rested, and Ellie hadn't returned when the afternoon slid over the land. Perhaps it was for the best, he smiled as he once again strolled through town to the blacksmith's shop. He checked the pinto's hooves and paid the man his price. "Fine job," he said.

The smith nodded in satisfaction. "Horse like that needs a fine job," the man said.

Fargo started to lead the Ovaro from the shop when he heard the voice, unmistakable in its determined sharpness.

"But I contracted with you for that horse," it said, and Fargo edged out farther to see Trudy Deakens standing, hands on her hips, in front of Malachy the horse dealer. "I gave you a deposit and told you I'd be back to pay the rest," she said.

Malachy had a round figure and a face to go with it in which small eyes almost hid behind wrinkles made of years of cagey self-protection. The man was a horse trader and his life was in his face. "I'm giving your deposit back to you. Here it is," he said, and pushed the bills at Trudy.

"I don't want the deposit. I want that horse. You'd no right to sell him with my deposit in your pocket," Trudy insisted. "Did you tell this buyer you'd taken a deposit on the horse?"

"I did. He told me he was buying the horse, anyway," Malachy said.

"Then he's no better than you are. Neither of you have any ethics or any honor," Trudy flung back.

Fargo saw Malachy's round face set itself and the man's eyes grow smaller. "Maybe not, but I've got my head on. A man doesn't say no to Bert Tooney," the man said.

"And so you just sell him my horse because he wanted it," Trudy snapped.

Fargo moved back deeper into the shop where he could still watch and listen but stay unseen.

"That's right. Now take your damn deposit back," Malachy said.

"You'd no right, no damn right at all. A deposit

seals a contract," Trudy snapped as she snatched the money from the man's hand.

"Don't bother me anymore about it, girl," Malachy said.

"Where will I find this Bert Tooney?" Trudy queried. "He has my horse and he'll sell him to me or I'll take him."

Malachy stared back at her in disbelief. "You plumb loco, honey?" he said.

"No, but I'm getting that horse back. You'd no right selling it and he had no right buying it," she returned.

"He'll be at the saloon after eight tonight. He plays cards there," Malachy said.

Fargo at last stepped forward as Trudy started to stride away. "Hold on a minute, Trudy Deakens," he said, and when she saw him, surprise flooded her face.

"You," she gasped. "Did you hear this?"

"I did, and I think maybe you'd best simmer down," Fargo said.

"Simmer down?" Trudy exploded. "Are you taking his side?"

"No. I just think there are some things best not rushed into," Fargo said patiently.

"I should just forget about the horse I bought and I need?" Trudy frowned.

"Might be the wisest thing," Fargo said.

"Well, you can forget that. I'm going to get that horse," she said, and stalked away, her tight rear jiggling as she stomped hard across the ground.

Fargo looked at Malachy and saw the man's small eyes glare back at him. "Little cactus, isn't she?" Fargo remarked.

"Bert Tooney'll take the needles out of her," the man grunted.

"She's right, you know. You'd no call to sell a horse you took money on," Fargo said.

"Don't preach to me, mister. I did what I had to do," he said.

Fargo's eyes held on the man. Malachy knew very well he'd done wrong. But to Malachy, honor was an indulgence, self-interest a reality. The world was full of those like him, men who couldn't understand that the two were connected.

"This Bert Tooney's a hard man, is he?" Fargo said.

"He likes killin' people who cross him the wrong way," Malachy said, and Fargo nodded, his lips pursed as he swung onto the Ovaro and walked the horse away.

It'd be a waste of time to stop by the Conestogas and talk to Trudy. She was too angry to listen and too stubborn to be sensible. But she could well get herself killed, he realized, or subject to a lot of other things she wouldn't enjoy. He drew a deep sigh and shook his head, almost in resignation, as he rode from town, found a tall red cedar, and made himself comfortable against its sweet-smelling bark. He closed his eyes, dozed, and woke again as the night came. He waited, let another hour go by, and swung onto the Ovaro.

This was absolutely the last time, Fargo muttered to himself. He'd put plenty of distance between himself and Trudy Deakens after tonight. He'd called her a pain in the ass. The description fit even more than he'd realized.

4

The saloon was only fairly crowded, the bar along one wall, a dozen tables on the other side of the room. Fargo, a shot glass of bourbon in one hand, had pressed himself into a corner where he was almost invisible but could see the entire room. Bert Tooney was already seated at one of the card tables, playing seven-card stud with four other men who had called out to him when he entered. Carefully watching the man walk to the table, Fargo took in a tall, thin figure, long arms, and long hands with thin, bony fingers. The man's walk was smooth and springy, his face lean, with a thin nose and icy blue eyes, a face that combined cruelty and craftiness.

Bert Tooney would kill quickly, Fargo realized. That much was in the man's eyes. But his extralong arms would get in the way of a really quick, smooth draw, Fargo took note, also, as he casually watched the cardplayers. Tooney was winning at the game, Fargo saw.

He was about to order another bourbon when the double doors swung open and Trudy Deakens strode into the saloon. She was the instant object of dozens of eyes as she halted in the center of the room. "I'm looking for Bert Tooney," she announced in a clear, firm voice, and the room fell almost silent.

Fargo's eyes went to Tooney and saw the man's

gaze go out to the young woman, who waited with her pretty face set.

"Over here, girlie," Tooney called out, and Trudy immediately strode over to the table. Fargo saw Tooney's cold eyes take in the curve of her body, linger on the very high, very round breasts.

"You have a horse that belongs to me," Trudy snapped. "I had a deposit on him and you'd no right buying him, and you know it."

"I bought him fair and square, girlie," Tooney said. He allowed a cold smile to cross his face as the others at the table looked on.

"Hell you did. Malachy told you I'd put a deposit on the horse," Trudy insisted.

Fargo rose and quietly made his way closer to the table but stayed behind Trudy, and he saw Bert Tooney's eyes narrow.

"You calling me a liar, girlie?" Tooney asked, his voice a thin growl.

"If the shoe fits, wear it," Trudy flung back, and Tooney's face darkened.

"You got a fresh mouth, bitch," Tooney said.

Trudy drew a roll of bills from her pocket and threw them on the table in front of the man. "That's what you paid for the horse. I'm taking him back," she said, and Fargo found himself torn between admiring her spitfire spunk and cursing her damn-fool stupidity.

Tooney swept the money from the table with his arm. "Pick it up and get out of here," he growled.

"I'm taking the horse," Trudy said.

"You're taking nothing, bitch," Tooney said. He began to rise to his feet.

"You going to shoot an unarmed girl?" Trudy asked. "Isn't that a little low even for you?"

"Goddamn you, I'll do something better than shoot you," Tooney rasped. "I'll have your little ass."

With a silent curse, Fargo saw Trudy step forward. "Win the horse and the money," she said. "I'll sit in for one hand. If I beat you, I take the horse and the money. You beat me, you get them both," she said, and Fargo watched Tooney hesitate. She'd done more than take him aback. She'd tossed him a challenge he'd have trouble fielding. If he brushed her aside, it'd look as though he were afraid, and if he took it, he might just lose and look worse for it.

Tooney's cruel mouth tightened. "Forget it. Anybody can get lucky for one hand," he said, a middle-of-the-road answer.

"We'll play three out of five wins," Trudy persisted, refusing to back away, and Tooney's glance took in the others looking on. He slowly lowered himself into the chair.

"Put your money in, bitch," he muttered, and Trudy bent down and scooped the bills from the floor. When she straightened up, someone had pushed a chair to the table for her and she sat down across from Tooney. "Just the two of us?" he asked.

"No. Seven-card's no good with just two players. The others can sit in," she said.

Two men leaned forward again and took their places at the table. All Trudy's attention remained on Bert Tooney, Fargo saw. She'd no idea he was almost directly behind her in the forefront of the crowd that had gathered to watch. The man next to Trudy began to deal and Fargo's eyes were narrowed as he watched every move that took place on the table.

Tooney won the first hand and allowed himself a thin smile. But Trudy knew how to play, Fargo saw. She was steady, read the face cards well. The second hand was dealt. Tooney won again and his smile grew broader.

"You want to quit and run now, girlie?" he slid at Trudy.

"Deal," she snapped at the third man. This time Trudy won with four sixes, and Tooney shrugged off the win. When she won the next hand with a ten-high diamond flush, his face had grown tight.

"You want to quit and run now?" Trudy said almost sweetly. She was pressing, showing not only fearlessness but contempt, and Fargo saw the cold fury in Tooney's eyes. The next deal would decide the winner and Fargo's glance held on the man's face. Tooney wasn't the kind to let himself lose to this brazen, disdainful girl. He might even explode some pretext to draw on her. But he'd not let himself lose, Fargo was certain, and his lake-blue eyes focused on the table, the cards and the hands of the players.

Trudy had her two down cards held close to herself and her first up card was an ace of spades. Fargo watched as Tooney's first up card was an ace of diamonds. The man beside Trudy drew a five, the fourth player a jack. The second round of up cards was dealt out, and Trudy drew a queen, Tooney a ten, the third player a seven, and the fourth a king. Trudy studied the cards faceup on the table and sat back as she received the third up card.

Fargo saw her make no effort to hide her smile when it turned out to be another queen. Tooney showed no expression and Fargo felt a stab of uneasiness at that. Tooney turned up a ten, the next man a two, and the fourth man a three. Fargo's eyes moved dartingly across the table as the players studied one another's up cards once again. He waited with them as the fourth up card was dealt, and he heard the gasp from those watching as Trudy drew another queen. She sat back, three queens faceup on the table.

Fargo watched the man next to her gather up his

cards. "That does me in," he said, and lifted his two hole cards momentarily before adding them to the others. Fargo glimpsed an ace in the two cards the man turned down, and his eyes went back to the table. Tooney drew a four and the other man still playing came up with a nine. He, too, folded his cards down when he saw the draw. "Hell, she's got three queens showing," he muttered. "She could have another one in the hole but I'm beat anyway." Fargo's gaze went to Tooney. The man remained unbothered.

"Last card," he murmured. "Down and dirty."

Fargo's eyes followed Trudy as she drew the last hole card and returned to Tooney, who had his three hole cards in his hands. Tooney's icy eyes were fastened on Trudy, his mouth a thin line. "Your call, girlie," he rasped.

Trudy took two of her hole cards and put them beside the three queens. "Full house, three queens and two tens," she said, and made no attempt to hide the triumph in her voice. "I'll be leaving with my horse now," she added.

"Hell you will, bitch," Tooney said, and an icy smile curled his lips as he put down all three of his hole cards. "Full house, three aces and two fours." Fargo watched Trudy stare at the man's card as astonishment, dejection, and defeat all flashed through her face. Fargo felt the furrow dig into his brow and he stared at the cards that had been laid out on the table, quick calculations racing through his mind. "My horse, my money, and I'm gonna take your little ass, too," Tooney said. "You lose it all."

"Not the way I see it," Fargo cut in, and saw Trudy spin in surprise while Bert Tooney's eyes grew narrow.

"Who the hell are you?" Tooney growled.

"Somebody who likes an honest game," Fargo said.

"You callin' me a cheat, mister?" Tooney said, and pushed his chair from the table, his eyes blazing.

Fargo stepped to the table, took up the cards the third player had turned down when he dropped out, and flipped them over. "When he folded, one of his down cards was an ace. The girl's got an ace faceup on the table, and now you show three more. That makes five aces in this deck as I count it," Fargo said. "You slipped the fifth one in, Tooney. You're a damn cheat."

Tooney went for his gun, leaping to his feet as he reached with his long, thin arm.

Fargo's Colt was out and firing before the man's gun had cleared its holster and Bert Tooney's long body folded forward almost in two as the heavy bullet ripped through his abdomen. He fell doubled over, hands clasped to his midsection, his head scraping the edge of the table as he went down and lay still.

Fargo turned to see Trudy staring at him, frozen in place and her mouth hanging open. She still managed to look pretty, he noted in passing. "You coming?" he asked, and the question snapped her out of the momentary spell.

She pulled her mouth closed, swallowed hard, scooped the money from the table, and hurried after him as he walked from the saloon. Outside, she paused beside the horse. "I'm taking the saddle off. I don't want to sit in it," she said, and quickly undid the cinch straps, pulled the saddle from the horse, and left it beside the hitching post. "Somebody will be happy to take it." She swung onto the horse's back. "Come with me to the wagons?" she said to Fargo. "We're camped just outside of town." He nodded and she led the way out of Beaver Falls and he spied the three Conestogas drawn up under a cluster of serviceberry. "I expect everyone will be asleep. I didn't tell anyone

I was going into town," she said, dismounting behind the wagons.

"I imagine not," Fargo commented. He slid from the Ovaro.

"I know you think it was stupid of me," she said, and managed to look both guilty and defiant.

"It sure as hell wasn't smart," Fargo answered.

"I know, if you hadn't been there, I'd have lost it all, and maybe a lot more," Trudy said. "Unless the man who had the ace in his hand would've seen something was wrong."

"Even if he'd figured that out, chances are he wouldn't have said anything. Tooney had a mean reputation, it seemed," Fargo said.

Trudy's deep-blue eyes stayed on him; she stepped forward, her arms sliding around his neck, and he was surprised as her mouth pressed hard against his, a kiss half-sweetness and half-sensuousness, a kiss on the edge of passion. The softness of her very round, very high breasts pressed into his chest, and his lips responded to the kiss until she pulled away.

"That a promise or a bribe?" he slid at her.

"It's a thank you for everything."

"Fair enough."

"I remember what you said when you left last time. I suppose what happened tonight only adds to that," she muttered.

"It does."

"I suppose it's stupid to ask you to stay on with us," Trudy said with a half-pout.

"It is."

"Dammit, you don't have to be so agreeable," she flared. "I guess this is the last time I'll be seeing you."

"It is if I have anything to do about it. A man could make a career out of pulling your chestnuts out of the fire, honey," Fargo said.

Her little shrug was an admission, and he pulled himself onto the Ovaro. "You're two people, Fargo," Trudy said, accusation in her voice. "One is brave, quick to help others and really very wonderful. The other is selfish, uncaring, and really very mean-spirited."

He laughed. She had her own ways of fighting. "Remember the one and watch the other ride off, honey," he said, and waved back as he sent the pinto into a slow trot.

He rode into the night and across a low hill and didn't look back. Maybe the succession of lessons was beginning to sink into Trudy Deakens, Fargo pondered. He had detected a touch less arrogant self-assurance in her. He hoped so, for her sake . . . and for the others in the three Conestogas. Maybe her uncle was wagon master but Trudy supplied the real strength. At another time he might have stayed on with her, Fargo smiled. Perhaps she'd grow to be really grateful. But he'd no time for further delays now, and he rode west until he grew tired, found a spot to camp for the night, and quickly slept.

When morning came on a bright, warm sun, he washed, dressed, and set the Ovaro northwest toward the foot of the Wind River Range. It took all day and into the night before he neared his destination, and he camped again, tiredness pulling at him. The following morning, after he was back in the saddle, he pulled into a cluster of blue spruce as he spied a line of near-naked horsemen move across his path. They stayed in the distance and finally vanished from sight. He moved on again and had gone another hour or so when he again pulled into a thicket of trees to watch another band of Indians riding hard. He watched until they vanished over a low hill.

Fargo moved from the thicket, carefully, headed onward, and slowed again as he saw a column of dust rise up to his left. He spurred the Ovaro onto a hill-ock, and a tiny furrow creased his brow as he watched a squad of blue-clad cavalry troops in a column of twos as they patrolled along a ridge. If they had seen the Indians, they weren't in pursuit, Fargo realized as he watched the troops vanish down the other side of the ridge.

He continued on his own path, rode a steady pace until he slowed again when he saw another patrol of some twenty troopers. He halted and waited as the troop rode toward him. A young-faced lieutenant rode at the head of the column and drew to a halt as he reached the lone horseman on the eye-catching Ovaro.

"Lieutenant Harrison, Third Cavalry," the young officer said. "You need help, mister?"

"Not exactly. I'm looking for Crooked Branch," Fargo said.

"About ten miles due north. You'll pass the garrison post just at the edge of town," the lieutenant said.

"Garrison?" Fargo frowned.

"That's right. Been quartered there for the past two years," the officer said. "You haven't visited Crooked Branch in some while, I guess."

"Never been there," Fargo said. "Spent enough time north in the Wind River Range but never got to Crooked Branch."

"Actually, most of our patrols go north into Wind River country," the lieutenant said. "We're just making a sweep down this way today."

"Saw another patrol earlier. You having trouble around here?" Fargo queried.

"There's always trouble around here. The major believes in patrols," the officer said.

"The major commands your garrison?" Fargo asked.

"That's right. Major Howard Thaxter," the trooper said.

"Much obliged, Lieutenant," Fargo said. He moved back as the platoon rode on. He watched them go out of sight and turned the pinto northwest, his eyes narrowed in thought as he put the pinto into a canter. He took a wide circle that let him go past the town and north into the Wind River Range. He had reached the base of the lush mountain range when he spotted a third patrol in the distance, riding hard, and he watched it go out of sight before continuing to move on deeper into the Wind River Range land.

The afternoon began to wear on when, at a distance, Fargo saw a fourth patrol, this time heading back toward Crooked Branch. The thoughts that had been sifting through his mind began to take shape and Fargo's lips tightened. He had seen four patrols, two south of town and two north. They were more than the ordinary deployment of a garrison's forces, and he scanned the land ahead of him.

The Wind River Range was Cheyenne country, where a garrison commander could be expected to send a platoon into the field to show presence if nothing else. But the four platoons he had seen had been searching, making wide, quick sweeps. A visit with Major Howard Thaxter might bring some answers, Fargo mused, but he decided to investigate on his own first. He still had a day or two to spare, and he turned the Ovaro up deeper into the Wind River land.

His eyes swept the soil as he rode, and he picked up the tracks of one of the cavalry platoons, hoofprints in a neat double row, unmistakably army tracks. He also saw the unshod tracks of numerous Indian ponies, some crisscrossing the prints of the platoon. He decided to follow the trail of pony prints and found himself moving higher into hills that were thick with trees yet held numerous passages wide enough for wagons. He followed the tracks that wound through trees and heavy shrub, moving into relatively open land that flattened out. He slowed as he saw the hoofprints of cavalry mounts break from thick brush and mingle in with the pony tracks. Frowning, Fargo followed the overlapping prints for another half-mile and then slowed as his nose picked up the slightly acrid scent of charred wood.

The Trailsman moved through a hedge of service-berry and reined to a halt to stare at the remains of four wagons that had been burned almost to the ground. The metal crossbows rose up like the bones of some strange skeleton, and the iron bands around the wheel were empty circles. Everything else was charred wood, some of it still smoldering.

Fargo scanned the ground and saw the pony tracks and the cavalry hoofprints mingled, crossing back and forth over one another. He dismounted, squatted down to peer harder at the prints, reading the markings, the patterns, the indentations, the way other men read words in a book. Finally he rose and scanned the scene again. There had been no pitched battle here. There were no deep marks in the ground, no long, skidding prints of horses sharply turned.

The unshod ponies had been here first, the Indian attack on the wagon quick and savage. The cavalry platoon had come upon the results later. There were no bodies in the charred remains of the wagons or outside, but Fargo picked up torn pieces of clothing on the ground. Some of the victims had leapt from the wagons as they tried to flee, but they had been quickly cut down. The Trailsman paused where three arrows were embedded into the ground and he pulled each one out separately and examined the wrapping on the sharp stones tips and the markings on the shaft of one. "Cheyenne," he grunted aloud, and moved on to where a line of footprints, heavy army boots, moved through a thick hedge of tall brush. He followed and came to a stop on the other side of the hedge, where he saw the row of freshly dug graves.

They added the last touch to the picture that had taken form in his mind. The cavalry platoon had formed a burial party, executed the grim task, and then regrouped and rode away, no doubt to report to the major. That explained the number of patrols he had seen. The major had quickly sent out squads in all directions to try to find the attackers.

A harsh laugh escaped Fargo's lips. The Cheyenne had long since gone their way and all the major's platoons were a waste of time and manpower.

Fargo walked back to the Ovaro and mounted the horse. Twilight had begun to drift down over the base of the range. But these low, rolling hills seethed with something more than the ordinary savagery. He felt it inside him, that extra sense he knew never to ignore, and he peered west across the land.

An old friend with the improbable name of Albert Two Pebbles lived in the low hills of the Wind River Range. Perhaps a visit to Albert might be informative, Fargo mused as he found a spot to bed down. Albert always knew the messages of man and beast and the ways of the forests, combining information and intuition, outer words and inner wisdoms. But a visit to town and perhaps Major Howard Thaxter was first, Fargo decided as he undressed and lay down on his bedroll. It was time to tend to his own affairs, he murmured inwardly as he let sleep roll over him in the darkness of the night.

5

When morning came, Fargo rose with the warm sun, washed, dressed, and found a stand of blueberries and luscious fox grapes; he took the time for a leisurely and satisfying breakfast.

The hills were lush and heavy with foliage as he finally rode down toward the more open land and headed for town. His lake-blue eyes scanned the terrain and he slowed as he saw a line of horsemen, the sun glistening on bodies shiny with fish oil. They were poised on a low hill and he counted ten in all. They had to see him as he saw them, and he prepared to put the Ovaro into a gallop when they turned and slowly went their way. He waited and made certain they wouldn't reappear in a flying charge and finally moved the Ovaro downward and onto the flat terrain.

He rode south and east and passed a few settlements as he drew closer to the town. When Crooked Branch came into view, he saw the garrison stockade just outside the buildings of the town itself. He slowed and took in a three-sided stockade with the barracks building forming the fourth side, the gate open wide, and three sentries atop the stockade wall. No major fort but a serviceable stockade, and he rode past and into Crooked Branch.

The town was something of a surprise, much neater than most such towns. It had the usual saloon and general store, but the streets seemed less rowdy and were filled with serious-faced people, many with heavily loaded supply wagons.

Fargo halted before a grizzled oldster lounging against a post. "There a hotel here in town?" he asked.

"Down the street some," the man said, and the Trailsman rode slowly on until the hotel appeared on his left, freshly painted, with a row of red geraniums across the front. He dismounted and went through a narrow doorway that barely permitted his shoulders to pass. A lobby opened up inside the door, a desk to one side where a man with thick eyeglasses glanced up.

"Come to see Oliver Kragg. He registered here?" Fargo asked.

"He is. Room Three, ground floor down the hall," the clerk said.

Fargo went down a wide corridor and found the room. The door was opened quickly at his knock and he faced a woman in a green dress with a low, square-cut bodice that barely contained heavy breasts. She let her eyes move up and down his powerful frame and her eyes finally held on the chiseled handsomeness of the big man in front of her.

"You must be Skye Fargo," she murmured.

"I am," he said. "But you're sure as hell not Oliver Kragg."

She smiled and he took in an attractive face with some thirty-five years on it, he guessed, little hints of lines around her brown eyes, a wide-cheekboned face, bottle-blond curly hair, and an animal sensuousness as obvious as the rouge on her cheeks that gave her more than an ordinary attractiveness. "I'm his secretary and traveling companion," she said in a low, husky voice that matched the sensuousness in her face. "Come in."

Fargo stepped into the room, almost touching the deep, heavy breasts with his arm as she only took a half-step back. He felt her eyes moving over him again, appraising, enjoying what she saw.

A man stepped from an adjoining room, a thin figure of medium height clothed in a brown suit and a shirt open at the neck. Fargo studied a nervous face, pale and pinched with nervous, constantly moving eyes.

"Oliver Kragg," the man said, and tried a broad smile that didn't hide the uneasiness in it. "I'm glad you're here. Now we can finish our agreement. Please sit down." He gestured to a chair as the woman eased herself into another chair across from him, the sensuous appraisal still in her eyes.

"I'm Elsa Cord," she said, and Fargo nodded back.

"Here's the rest of the four hundred, Fargo," Oliver Kragg said, producing a roll of bills and pushing it at the big man.

Fargo folded the money into his hand. "Spell it all out," he muttered.

"Six wagons. You'll break trail for them through the Wind River Range north to Jackson Hole," Kragg said.

"That's the heart of Cheyenne country." Fargo frowned. "You want to get there alive you'll go west past the Salt River Range and then north."

"I'll also lose weeks, and I can't afford that," Kragg said. "I'm meeting a man in Jackson Hole, a rich man who deals in land speculation. I made a promise to the folks in those wagons I have to keep."

Fargo's frown stayed. Oliver Kragg didn't seem the type who'd risk his neck because of a promise. "What kind of a promise?" Fargo questioned.

"The man I'm meeting wants to settle the land around Jackson Hole. We agreed that if I brought him the settlers who'd stay and work the land, he'd pay them each a thousand dollars," Kragg said.

"Mighty generous," Fargo commented.

"It's not generosity, it's foresight. If he gets a real

community going, he figures to open a bank and a trading post and make real money for himself. But he can't build a community without settlers. These six wagons will just be the first group. I'm to get others in time."

"For a fee, I take it," Fargo said.

"Yes, and for a piece of tomorrow," Kragg said.

Fargo found himself again thinking that this nervous, darting-eyed man didn't seem the kind to harbor grandiose dreams of building communities. But perhaps he was misjudging the man, he allowed. "Why the rush?" he asked.

"The man's leaving to go back East for the winter. He wants this group contracted and settled in before he leaves. Elsa here will draw up all the agreements when we get there. But it's a deadline I have to meet," Oliver Kragg said. "Not for myself so much but for the once-in-a-lifetime chance these settlers are getting. That's the promise I made to them, and I'm going to keep it."

"It's more a promise to get them killed going straight through Cheyenne country," Fargo said.

"Of course there's danger, I know that, but that's why I'm paying you the kind of money I am to take us through."

"I'll have to think more on it," Fargo muttered.

"You made the agreement when you took the advance money, Fargo," Kragg answered.

"I heard you were the kind of man who kept his word," Elsa cut in, and Fargo glanced at her and saw a quiet, almost amused light in her eyes.

"You heard right," Fargo answered. "But I'd feel better about it if I spoke to these settlers myself. I'd like to tell them what I think they're facing in my own words."

"You can do that, Fargo," Kragg said. "The last of the six wagons just arrived early this morning."

"After I make another visit," Fargo said.

"Elsa and I will be here whenever you're ready to go talk to them," Oliver Kragg said with a show of cooperation and magnanimity. The man's nervousness was a deep part of him, Fargo decided, and not tied in to any specific thing.

Elsa Cord rose and went to the door with him as Kragg disappeared into the other room. "It'll be fine trip, you wait and see," the woman said.

"That a prediction or a promise?" Fargo said blandly, and a small smile opened her full red lips.

"A little of both," Elsa Cord answered in her low, husky voice, which radiated sensuousness.

Fargo smiled and brushed past her as he went into the hall. Maybe Elsa Cord was unsatisfied or maybe she'd do anything to help Kragg's cause, Fargo wondered, or maybe she was simply a woman of unbounded appetite. He'd be finding out in time, he was certain.

Outside, he climbed onto the Ovaro and rode back through the town to the stockade. He passed through the open gate under the eyes of the two sentries on the wall and saw a busy garrison post, horses being groomed, troopers seeing to their equipment, and he saw a barracks and stable for a sizable force. The company pennant flew over the low roof of a small building near the barracks. Fargo rode to it and dismounted. A corporal by the door snapped to attention.

"Want to see the major," Fargo said. He waited as the man went inside to return moments later.

"Go in," the soldier said, and Fargo stepped into a small, neat office, a territory map on one wall, a wood file cabinet against another, and a small desk and two chairs in the center of the room. The man behind the desk rose, a trim figure, medium height in a crisply pressed uniform. Fargo took in piercing gray eyes and short-cropped black hair, a taut, intense face that exuded a disciplined tension as it took his measure with a long, probing stare.

"You're not from around here," the major said.

"That's right," Fargo answered. "Just passing through."

"Your name, mister?" the major asked. He had a way of making everything he said sound like an order, Fargo noted.

"Fargo, Skye Fargo. Some call me the Trailsman," the big man answered, and saw the major's narrowed stare grow narrower.

"I've heard about you," Major Thaxter said. "What can I do for you?"

"Tell me about the trouble you're having with the Cheyenne," Fargo said.

"No trouble, Fargo. Nothing more than usual, that is," Major Thaxter said.

"You had four patrols out yesterday. Isn't that a little unusual?" Fargo probed.

"I believe in heavy patrol activity," the major said. "Everyone in town knows that and it makes them feel secure."

"They know about the attack on those four wagons?" Fargo pushed at him, and saw the moment of surprise flash through the major's taut, disciplined face. "One of your platoons buried the victims," Fargo added.

Major Thaxter brought surprise under quick control and held his face stiffly formal. "No, I haven't made any announcement of it, if that's what you mean."

"I'd guess telling folks would be the proper thing to do," Fargo said.

"I see nothing to be gained by it," the major said stiffly. "No one on that wagon train was from here, no relatives or connections in this community. People here know the Cheyenne are a constant threat. There's no need to frighten them with more such examples."

"Seems to me the folks on other wagon trains would appreciate knowing. Might make them change their minds or take a different route," Fargo said. "There's a train waiting for me to go out with them and break trail."

"Yes, Oliver Kragg's wagons. I've spoken to Kragg and to his wagon master already," Major Thaxter said.

"You tell them about that attack yesterday?" Fargo pressed, and the officer didn't hide the annoyance that rose inside him.

"I told you, I don't believe in frightening people unneccessarily," the major said. "And I don't appreciate my considered judgment being questioned by you."

"I've no problem with frightening people," Fargo snapped. "I'm sure as hell going to tell them what I saw."

Major Thaxter's eyes became frosted pinpoints of gray. "You're free to do whatever you please," he said. "But I suggest you watch your words. This territory is under my command and I won't stand for myself or my troops being maligned."

"I'll remember that," Fargo said. He strode from the small office to where he'd left the Ovaro outside. The major had tried to let stiff-backed formality and thinly veiled threats cloak answers that had been weak and unresponsive. The question was why, Fargo pondered as he rode from the stockade. There had to be reasons but the major wouldn't be volunteering any, Fargo grunted, and his thoughts swirled as he rode the pinto westward.

The Indian attack was nothing unusual of itself, but the major's reaction remained as questionable as his attitude. Fargo found himself wondering if the truth lay somewhere out in the untamed wildness. If so, one man would know . . . Fargo turned the Ovaro into the foothills of the Wind River Range.

6

Fargo rode unhurriedly, the day already well into the afternoon, and he realized he might well have to wait till morning to reach Albert Two Pebbles. The forest land grew more dense with heavy stands of box elder and gambel oak. Fargo's eyes never stopped searching the land on all sides as he rode. He'd been riding for over an hour after climbing to a long, broad rise when his wild-creature hearing caught the faint sound of a rein chain. The sound came from some dozen yards ahead and eliminated it being an Indian pony, but Fargo moved cautiously nonetheless. Finally he spied two riders moving along the rise in front of him. He frowned as he watched the two men. They weren't simply riding along the rise. They were following someone, moving carefully, slowing, then quickening their pace, and all the while leaning forward in the saddle as they peered ahead.

Fargo moved closer, near enough to glimpse their faces, one long and lean, the other square and heavy-jawed. One of the two men kept glancing down the side of the rise, and Fargo brought his gaze downward, peering hard through the trees. Finally he spotted the three horsemen moving along a trench at the bottom of the slope. They rode carefully, stayed parallel to the two horsemen atop the rise, and Fargo's eyes narrowed in thought. They were moving in a way designed for only one kind of maneuver, and curious,

Fargo turned the pinto from the rise and rode upward onto a hill above the two riders. He sent the pinto forward and went past the two men below him, continued on as he scanned the rise until he spotted the lone horseman moving through the trees below.

The rider moved into a break in the trees where the sun streamed down, and Fargo heard the gasp of surprise fall from his lips as he saw the shock of flame-red hair first, then the copper sheen of the magnificent palomino. "I'll be dammed," he breathed as he stared at the redheaded rider below. "Canyon O'Grady."

The images exploded in his mind, too recent to be called memories. It had only been months since Canyon O'Grady had saved his scalp from a particularly nasty band of bucks and then stayed around to help him get at the truth about a brothel that specialized in kidnapped girls. He'd been a charming rogue, with the skills to back up his charm, and the ability to say a lot without saying anything at all. But he'd been special, the kind of man you didn't forget, and Fargo sent the pinto forward through the trees, past the redheaded rider below.

When he'd gone far enough, he swerved sharply and sent the horse down the short slope to come out of the trees a few feet in front of the horseman. He saw the Colt New Model Army pistol with ivory grips leveled at him, an accurate, fast-firing weapon, six-shot single action.

"Hold up, now, that's no way to greet a friend." Fargo smiled and watched the astonishment flood the big man's face.

"I'll be dammed," Canyon O'Grady gasped.

"My sentiments exactly," Fargo agreed.

"Fargo," the red-haired man said, incredulousness still in his crackling blue eyes.

"Canyon O'Grady"—the Trailsman laughed—"what in hell are you doing out here?"

"I'm looking for a chap," the flame-haired man said, and Fargo smiled at the lilt in the man's voice. He'd forgotten how it added a dash of charm to everything O'Grady said.

"Somebody hiding out here in these hills?" Fargo asked.

"Maybe not exactly in these hills," O'Grady said with a diffident smile. "But someplace in these parts. At least that's what my instincts tell me."

"I've something your instincts didn't tell you," Fargo said as he edged his horse closer to the palomino.

"If you mean those two clods trailing me, I know they're there." The big redheaded man grinned. "I've been waiting for them to make their move. I thought you were one of them coming down the hill. I spotted them a good while back."

"Did you spot the other three down below?" Fargo asked, and enjoyed how Canyon's O'Grady's roguish face darkened with surprise.

"I did not," O'Grady said. "I'll be thanking you for that."

"They're getting ready to catch you in between them," Fargo said.

O'Grady's lips pursed in thought. "So it would seem."

"They expect you'll see the two up here when they come at you. While you're concentrating on them, the other three will bring you down from behind and below in a cross fire. They're just waiting for the right spot, I imagine."

Canyon O'Grady allowed a wry smile. "This does put a different face on things."

"We turn their plan around on them. First, you pick the spot," Fargo said, and Canyon's eyes waited. "The two following up here are watching us by now. We'll let them see a chance meeting of old friends."

"True enough so far," Canyon said.

"We shake hands and you go on your way while I go on mine. I ride back the other way. They'll watch me go by and then go on after you. Meanwhile, I turn down into the trench and tail the other three. When they make their move on you, I'll do to them what they were going to do to you: hit them from the rear."

"While I take care of the other two." Canyon smiled. "Neat."

Fargo drew the horse back a pace, laughed loudly, made an elaborate exhibition of shaking hands with the big flame-haired man, and then turned the Ovaro away. "Good to see you again, Canyon," he called back, and followed with a wave of his hand. He rode casually along the top of the rise.

The two men had faded back into the trees, but he was safe, he knew. They'd no reason to attack him, but more important, they knew shots would alert their quarry and they'd not want that.

Fargo rode on, aware the two men watched him pass from behind the thick foliage, and when he'd gone far enough, he turned the pinto down the slope of the rise and came out in the trench below.

He hurried forward, this time peering ahead for the three riders, and he spied them after a few minutes just as they halted. He moved in as close as he dared, and when they dismounted, he slid from the Ovaro and dropped to one knee. He glanced up at the top of the rise and saw that Canyon O'Grady had halted at a spot where there was a wide break in the tree line.

Fargo smiled. The two attackers following would have to come into the clear to attack. They'd never make it halfway across, he wagered. He drew his own Colt and rose to a crouch to move forward after the three men, who had begun to climb up the slope. They stayed pretty much in a line, Fargo noted, and he saw they'd drawn their guns. They'd wait for the shooting to erupt on the rise before pouring gunfire up the slope. Fargo's gaze went past them to the rise where he saw Canyon, halted, his head bent down as if he were trying to light a cigarette.

When the first shot rang out, Fargo saw Canyon almost disappear as he went down headfirst from the side of his saddle. The two horsemen came into sight racing across the open space, and the palomino half-bolted to reveal Canyon O'Grady on one knee, his ivory-gripped Colt spitting bullets. Fargo glimpsed both of the attackers go down, but his attention was on the three men in front of him. The one in the center was first to bring his gun up, but he never got a shot off as Fargo's bullet slammed into the back of his neck. The man drove forward, his face smashing into the ground as if pinned there by an invisible lance. Both of the other two men spun, astonishment in their faces.

Fargo chose the one to the right, and the Colt barked again. The man gave a convulsive quiver as a gusher of red erupted just below his throat and his body began to half-slide, half-roll down the slope. Fargo brought his attention back to the third man, who was half-twisting, half-rolling down the slope at an angle. The man found a line of low shrub to roll behind and Fargo held up his shot, glanced up at the top of the rise, where he saw Canyon O'Grady standing over the two motionless forms.

Fargo looked back to the brush, which shook as the man hurriedly crawled down the slope. He was making for the horses, Fargo saw, and he rose to one knee and waited, the Colt ready to fire. The line of brush led all the way down to where the horses waited, but the fleeing attacker would have to come into the clear when he mounted his horse. The line of brush shook again, almost at the three horses now, and Fargo lifted the Colt as he saw the horses move, then a brown mare backed away from the others.

"Shit," he swore, and rose to his feet, the Colt still aimed. But the man had been more clever than he'd expected, Fargo saw. Staying on the far side of the horse, he'd sent the mount racing away while he clung with one foot in the stirrup and his arms around the horse's neck from below. Fargo caught a glimpse of him clinging precariously to the horse but nonetheless clinging as the mare vanished into the trees. He sent a shot after the fleeing horse, more out of frustration than anything else.

"Forget it," he heard the voice say and turned to see Canyon O'Grady coming toward him down the slope, leading the palomino behind him. "We'll not be seeing him again," Canyon added. "Now the shoe's on the other foot, friend. It's you doing the favors," he added with the wide and charming grin that was a part of him.

"One good turn deserves another," Fargo said as the big flame-haired man walked with him to where he'd left the Ovaro. "Who were they?"

"A handful of bad losers," Canyon said. "I beat them in a poker game and took their IOUs and said I'd be back to collect. It seems they decided to see that I never did."

Fargo smiled inwardly. Canyon O'Grady had proved himself good with quick, glib answers during their last meeting, and he was doing it again. This was a big, wild country. Men who'd given bad IOUs had only to take off and disappear. It wasn't likely they'd tail somebody for miles and miles to make sure they'd the perfect place to bring him down. But he let the answer go for the moment. "No connection, then, with the man you're trying to find?" he asked.

"None at all." Canyon smiled, and Fargo nodded while he took the answer with another grain of salt. "And what brings you out roaming these hills, Fargo?" the man asked.

"Out to find an old friend who is part of the Wind River Range," Fargo answered, and watched O'Grady's snapping blue eyes sweep the lush and rolling hills.

"Wind River, Lost Trail Pass, Medicine Bow, Spirit Creek, Massacre Canyon, Big Smokey, such wonderful names you have in this land," Canyon intoned, almost a reverence in his voice. "You know, they say the heart of a people is in the names of the land, and in America your names are strong, rugged, deep with roots. They fly like the eagle and yet are rock-solid."

"You're a poet, O'Grady," Fargo commented.

"Did you ever see an Irishman who wasn't?"

Fargo laughed and glanced at the long shadows of dusk that had begun to slide across the land. "Let's get away from here and find a spot to camp. I won't be finding my friend till morning," he said. He led the way along the trench, found a passage that rose into higher land, and halted in a glen of chestnut. "Cold beef strips do?" he asked, and Canyon nodded.

"They'll do fine. I've some oatmeal biscuits we can add," he said, and stretched out as night descended and a half-moon appeared in the blue velvet sky.

"If you like names, you'll like my friend Albert Two Pebbles," Fargo remarked.

"I like him already. I take it he's Indian," Canyon said.

"Some Cheyenne, some Arapaho, some fur trader. Albert used to act as a kind of messenger between the old Fifth Cavalry from Fort Hall across the border in

72

Oregon Territory and the tribes that bordered the Wind River."

"This just a social visit?" Canyon asked between bites of the beef strips.

"Not exactly. I'm here to break trail for a wagon train smack through the Cheyenne country. But something's going on, I can feel it in my bones," Fargo said.

"Purely instinct?" O'Grady smiled, skepticism in the question and the smile.

"No. There's a garrison at Crooked Branch with a major who sends out extra heavy patrol platoons, keeps the massacre of a wagon train under his hat while insisting there's nothing beyond the usual going on. It doesn't smell right," Fargo said, and recounted his visit with Major Thaxter.

Canyon O'Grady's lips were pursed in thought when he finished. "You're right, it doesn't smell right," O'Grady agreed.

"Maybe Albert can shed some light on it," Fargo said. "You're welcome to come along."

"I might do that," Canyon said as he took down his bedroll and stretched out on it. "And if you can use some help at anything, just call on me. I owe you for what you did back on the rise."

"I'll keep that in mind," Fargo said.

O'Grady shed his gun belt and clothes, revealing a powerfully muscled chest and torso, skin that took only a light tan and legs with the sinews of a small oak. He was one of those men who looked bigger with his clothes off than on.

"Sleep well, lad," O'Grady said as he lay down.

"And you," Fargo murmured, closing his eyes at once and letting slumber sweep him up.

The night stayed quiet, with only the soft night sounds murmuring in the stillness, and Fargo slept soundly until the dawn broke over the high peaks and the sun cast a net of waking warmth over the land.

The Trailsman rose and was dressed when O'Grady sat up and rubbed sleep from his eyes.

"Been riding almost the last two days," the man said. "I could sleep another dozen hours."

"Sorry, I have to move on," Fargo said, and O'Grady mumbled as he hurriedly dressed.

Fargo led the way west deeper into the base hills, halted to wash and let the horses drink at a fast-flowing stream, and then moved on again. He cast a glance over at the flame-haired man who rode alongside him with casual calm.

"You said you were looking for someone. Why?" Fargo asked.

"Some people have lost a lot of money. They feel he may know something about it and they asked me to find him," Canyon said.

It was another answer that offered a reason couched in vagueness. Fargo smiled. "You know, Canyon O'Grady, for a man that talks a lot you say very little," he commented, and frowned in admiration at how hurt O'Grady managed to look.

"With all I've told you about myself?" Canyon said.

"Oh, you've told me how your pa left Ireland in the potato famine, and with a price on his head for revolutionary connections," Fargo said. "And you told me how he worked building the railroads back East but that wasn't for you. But there's damn little else I know about you. You're no ordinary cowhand. You're a crack shot and you carry a Colt with ivory grips. You could be a gunslinger, but you don't have the eyes for it. You ride an exceptionally fine horse, but you're no wrangler. Never saw a wrangler with an outfit neat and well-kept as yours. You're no trapper or mountain man. You don't carry the gear for the first or roar like the second. Just what the hell are you, Canyon O'Grady?"

"A wanderer, a tinker, a man of odd jobs." Canyon smiled, taking in the accurate analysis with unfazed good spirits.

"What kind of odd jobs?" Fargo pressed.

"Whatever suits my fancy . . . or my pocketbook."

Fargo cast a long, probing glance at the man riding beside him. "Why don't I believe a damn word of that?" he asked.

"Could be you're just a skeptical man at heart, my friend," Canyon replied affably.

"Could be I'm right," Fargo muttered.

Canyon's laugh had a lilt in it. "We'll just leave it at that."

"For now," Fargo grunted. He spurred the Ovaro into a trot as they approached a narrow passage of rock at one side and a line of Rocky Mountain maples. It was the mark he'd been looking for. At the end of the passage the land dipped and at the bottom of the small hollow sat a log cabin with the canvas lean-to attached to one side for a livestock shelter.

Fargo rode to a halt, Canyon a half-pace behind. The figure that stepped from the cabin was long, lean, and clothed in a pair of baggy black trousers and a black, round-peaked hat. His chest was bare except for a string of onyx stones, and he watched Fargo swing down from the Ovaro with his lined face impassive. Only the glint in his black eyes betrayed the stoniness of his visage.

"Should I expect the trees to fall?" he asked.

"All right, it's been a long time. I just haven't been this way. I'm glad to see you still have that sideways sense of humor, old friend," Fargo said.

A fleeting change in the impassive face might have

been a smile. "You have not changed either, Fargo," the man said.

Canyon swung down from the palomino as Fargo dismounted and gestured to the impassive-faced man. "This is my old friend Albert Two Pebbles," he introduced. "This one calls himself Canyon O'Grady."

Albert Two Pebbles nodded at O'Grady and returned his gaze to Fargo. "You haven't come just to look at this old face," he said.

"I might have," Fargo protested.

"Yes, you might have, but you haven't. Something has brought you to the Wind River Mountains," Albert said.

"A wagon train," Fargo conceded. "I'm to break trail for them straight through Cheyenne country." He saw the faint shrug that touched Albert's shoulders. "Something bothers me about it."

"There is never a good time for that, but it is especially bad now," Albert said.

"Why? I keep getting signals I can't pin down," Fargo said. "I've seen too many patrols I don't understand, heard too many answers that don't sit right."

"You spoke to the major at the garrison," Albert said, and again the hint of a smile touched his face. "He told you nothing because he is in a war with Strongarrow, chief of the Wind River Cheyenne."

"A war?" Fargo frowned

"A battle between them. A special hate. You have another word for it I cannot remember," Albert said.

"I think he means feud," Canyon put in, and Albert Two Pebbles nodded.

"Strongarrow would kill every soldier and settler to destroy the major," he said. "The major would wipe out all the Cheyenne to kill Strongarrow."

"There's a damn-sight more likelihood of the first than the second, I'd say," Canyon remarked.

"This is dangerous-enough country without a damn personal feud added," Fargo snapped out. "Thaxter's got no business getting himself into this kind of thing. That explains why he's keeping quiet about that wagon massacre. It's not that he doesn't want to frighten people; he doesn't want to admit the Cheyenne's one up on him."

"Sounds like the major has an obsession about this Cheyenne chief," Canyon commented. "Obsessions are always dangerous. They destroy a man's soul."

"You're being a poet again," Fargo said. "I don't give a damn about the major's soul. I'm concerned with his judgment."

"Obsessions destroy both," Canyon said.

Fargo turned to Albert Two Pebbles. "You have any wise words under your hat, Albert?" he asked grimly.

"No one steps in a hornet's nest without being stung," Albert said calmly.

"Hah! I'm not the only poet," the Irishman roared. "I'd say he's telling you to back away from all of this." Fargo's lips pursed in thought for a long moment. "You going to have trouble with that?" Canyon asked.

"Maybe. Some insist I gave my word," Fargo said. "I'll think more on it." He turned and pulled himself onto the Ovaro and turned to the slender, stoic figure of Albert Two Pebbles. "Thank you, old friend," he said. "Stay well."

"It will be easier for me than for you," Albert said laconically.

"A good day to you," Canyon called back as he rode after Fargo and came up alongside him. "Back to Crooked Branch for you?" he asked.

"That's right."

"Good. We can ride into town together," Canyon said. "I'll be paying a visit to the local saloon, maybe more than one. There's no place like a saloon for picking up information."

"Then you don't think your man will be in town," Fargo said.

"Can't say. Most likely not but he could be. Luck might smile on me."

"What makes you think he's in these parts?"

"He's the kind that might need a town," Canyon replied.

"A gambling man, is he?" Fargo slid out.

"I didn't say that, but there might be some truth to it."

Fargo smiled. It was another of O'Grady's evasive answers. He led the way over a rise and down a hill thick with hackberry. His jaw grew tight as Canyon rode easily beside him and he moved the pinto through the trees in a twisting, turning path.

"That Albert's too damn good a prophet," he muttered, caught the quizzical glance Canyon threw at him. "He said it'd be easier for him to stay well than us," Fargo added.

"Do I interpret that to mean we have company?"

"Bull's-eye," Fargo grunted.

"I've been feeling it, only I wasn't sure if I was just letting my imagination run off, the feeling of someone else in these hills with us," Canyon said.

"Four someones. I spotted them when we started down. They're behind us now." Fargo's eyes were narrowed as they swept the terrain ahead. "They'll be charging any minute. They'll separate when they do, to come at us from all sides."

"I'd suggest we take their targets away from them," the flame-haired man said almost casually.

"In there," Fargo agreed, and pointed to a dense tangle of tall brush.

"Good. They'll have to come in after us, and that puts the shoe on the other foot," Canyon said.

Fargo broke off anything further as the high-pitched war whoop cracked the air and the sound of racing hoofbeats rolled down the hill. He glanced to his left and glimpsed the flashing horsemen racing through the trees. He spurred the Ovaro toward the thick brush, the palomino racing beside him neck and neck. When he reached the dense brush and two arrows hurtled past his head, he swerved the Ovaro sharply to the left as he leapt from the saddle, both legs stretched out straight. He glimpsed Canyon O'Grady swerve in the opposite direction as he leapt from the palomino. Fargo used his forearms to shield his face as he landed in the densely tangled brush and rolled until the branches stopped his momentum.

He heard Canyon land hard in the brush at the other end, and he rose on one knee, whirled, the Colt in hand, and saw the Cheyenne charging into the brush. Two charged in from west to east and two from north to south. They'd lowered their short bows and brought out long-bladed hunting knives and tomahawks as they leaned from their ponies to sweep the tangled branches.

A bony-framed buck swerved and charged directly at where Fargo hid, and the sturdy Indian pony crashed through the dense brush without slowing. Fargo held himself in place long enough to draw a direct bead, and when he fired, the bony figure seemed to disintegrate in all directions as the heavy bullet tore through its chest. Fargo saw a second buck passing near, riding from the other direction and bouncing strangely on his horse. Only when he passed did Fargo see the unmistakable handle of a bowie knife protruding from the small of his back.

As the Cheyenne toppled from the horse, Fargo saw a third buck leap into the brush and disappear. The

Colt barked but the shot was too late. He heard the fourth Cheyenne at the opposite end of the thick, tangled brush, but that'd be Canyon O'Grady's concern. Fargo stayed on one knee, the Colt ready to fire, and strained his ears to pick up a sound from the Cheyenne. But he heard none, though he was certain the buck wasn't lying in silent fear. The Cheyenne was on the attack and he'd not sit back. Fargo's eyes were narrowed as they scanned the tangle of branches, leaves, and tough, earthbound vines.

A faint wind rippled through the leaves and he cursed silently as it robbed him of a chance to track his foe's movements. He was still peering slowly across the brush in front of him when he caught the faint sound, a sudden swish of air. He flung aside the impulse to whirl and fire, and instead dived forward. But the tomahawk that hurtled through the air managed to catch him a glancing blow along the back of the head, enough to make the world explode in a shower of red and yellow flashes. He felt himself hit the ground, facedown, his head still exploding; and somehow, drawing from an inner reserve of strength, he managed to whirl and fire. He emptied the gun, seeing only grayness, trusting to luck as he sprayed shots. He rolled and shook his head, and the curtain of grayness partly lifted as he felt powerful hands close around his throat. He felt himself pulled backward and down, and fighting out of habit and conditioning, he reached both arms up, hands groping, found two fistfuls of greased black hair, and pulled.

He heard the yelp of pain and the hands around his throat were snatched away to grab at his wrists. Fargo shook his head again and the half-gray curtain lifted as the Indian pulled hands from his hair. Fargo yanked his arms back, half-rolled, wrapped his arms around the Cheyenne's leg, and pulled again. The Indian went down with a guttural curse and Fargo saw blood streaming from the man's side. One of his shots had hit, he realized, and he rolled, got to his feet, and felt the blood on his own temple. The Cheyenne was rushing at him again but he saw the Indian was weakened, fighting out of the strength of hate.

The Cheyenne raised one arm and Fargo saw the hunting knife in his hand. The Indian half-leapt, half-stumbled forward to bring the knife down, but Fargo's left arm shot out, his hand closing around the red man's wrist while he brought his right up in a driving hook that almost whistled. It landed flush on the Indian's jaw and Fargo heard the crack of his jawbone. The Cheyenne stiffened for a moment, shook, and collapsed into a heap.

Fargo reached down, took the hunting knife from the hand that still gripped it, and flung it into the brush. He dropped to one knee and the pain shot through his temple as, with a grimace, he pressed his kerchief against the side of his face. It had all happened with only half-realized awareness after the tomahawk blow, and now he took time for a deep breath of relief.

Canyon O'Grady's voice interrupted his thoughts as the man called his name.

"Over here," Fargo said. He looked up to see the Irishman push through the tangled brush toward him.

"You had a bit of a close one," Canyon said as he halted.

"Too close. He was barefoot and circled behind me more quickly than I expected he could," Fargo said, pushing to his feet and gazing at O'Grady. "You look as though you didn't draw a deep breath."

"I didn't. My two didn't make a smart move between them," Canyon said. "Let's get the horses and find a stream to clean off that head of yours."

Fargo nodded and held the kerchief to his throbbing temple with one hand as he walked to the Ovaro and pulled himself into the saddle. He gripped the reins with one hand and let Canyon lead the way across the low hills until they came to a clear, fast-running brook; he bathed the kerchief in the cold water and cleaned the side of his face.

The tomahawk had been a glancing-blow, yet it had put a gash in the top of his temple just at the hairline, he saw, and after cleaning the wound, he applied a salve from a small vial in his saddlebag. "Yarrow, comfrey, and lemon balm," he gold Canyon, who looked on with fascination.

"I carry a few things, but not that one. I must include it," Canyon said as Fargo rose, finished washing out the kerchief, and returned to the saddle.

"Let's get to town before we have any more delays," he said, and Canyon swung in beside him.

Fargo set a steady pace and the day had passed into late afternoon when he reached the edge of Crooked Branch. Canyon slowed to a halt. "The saloon's in the middle of town," Fargo said. "I'll be stopping off before then."

"You'd best remember Albert Two Pebbles' advice, my friend," Canyon said.

"I'll remember it, whether I can take it or not," Fargo said.

"Why don't you meet me for a drink tomorrow night? I'd like that before we go on our separate ways."

"And you can tell me how you're doing finding this man you're after who might or might not be in town and might or might not be a gambling man," Fargo speared with a grin.

Canyon O'Grady's roguish face broke into a laugh.

"Fair bargain," he said, and sent the palomino into a fast trot.

Fargo moved on slowly and considered another visit to Major Thaxter, mostly for his own satisfaction. The man deserved to have his lies flung into his face. But that could wait. There were other things to do first and he drew up before the hotel, dismounted, and strode to Oliver Kragg's room.

The man opened the door at his knock and Fargo saw Elsa Cord there. Her eyes met his at once, the same inviting sensuousness behind their brown orbs.

"I was getting worried about you, Fargo," Kragg muttered.

"I wasn't." Elsa Cord smiled, and Fargo returned the smile as her eyes held his.

"I've more to say now to the people in those wagons of yours," Fargo said to Kragg.

"Let's go see them," Kragg said with an equanimity that took Fargo by surprise. He followed the man out of the hotel still wrestling with a combination of surprise and uneasiness.

7

Kragg unhitched a sturdy brown horse from the post outside the hotel and led the way just beyond the other end of town, where Fargo saw the six wagons in a half-circle. "They're all here and waiting," Kragg said, and came to a halt at the wagons, all big, heavy Conestogas, Fargo noted.

Figures began to emerge from the wagons as he dismounted and Kragg called out in a strong voice. "This is the Trailsman, friends. He's going to take us through to our destination."

Fargo watched still others come from the Conestogas and felt himself staring at the trim, black-haired figure that came toward him, very high, very round breasts swaying faintly, and behind her, the worn-faced man that carried perpetual defeat in his eyes.

"No," Fargo heard himself breath aloud. "Christ, no."

"You're the Trailsman," Trudy Deakens said, brows arching. "Well, this is a surprise."

"Not one I like," Fargo grunted, and turned to Kragg. "She going to be part of this train?" He frowned.

"Yes, Ben Deakens's the wagon master," Kragg said.

"Then you can definitely count me out," Fargo said.

"Now, wait a minute," Kragg said. "What's this all about?"

"It's about not being fair," Trudy snapped with

angry defensiveness in her voice. "It's about being a bastard."

Fargo pointed at her. "She attracts trouble like a pile of manure attracts flies," he said.

"That's not so, not really," Trudy shot back, and managed to sound hurt as well as angry.

"On top of that, she won't listen or take orders," Fargo said.

"Everybody's entitled to a mistake," Trudy said.

"You're making a career out of them, honey," Fargo said.

"You can settle your differences among yourselves," Kragg said. "Your opinion of Miss Deakens doesn't change the fact that you made an agreement to take these wagons through."

Fargo settled a hard glare on Oliver Kragg and saw the man swallow nervously. "It's not important," Fargo said, and turned to the others. "You'd be crazy to go through the Wind River Range. The Cheyenne are on the warpath. I came on four wagons they massacred a few days ago. On top of that, Major Thaxter's in a running feud with the Cheyenne chief." He halted, his eyes sweeping those who listened. They were serious, polite, and he saw, unmoved.

"We're going through, Fargo," Ben Deakens said. "There's a thousand dollars waiting for each family if we reach Jackson Hole in time. We're not turning away from that."

"Your lives are worth more than a thousand dollars and some homestead land, for God's sake," Fargo shot back.

"We're going to be quite safe," Trudy put in smugly. "We've been assured of that."

Fargo frowned in disbelief at her. "Assured of that? Who in hell have you been listening to, honey? The Good Fairy?"

"Major Thaxter," Oliver Kragg answered.

"What?" Fargo blurted.

"That's right. The major assured us we'd be safe," Kragg said.

"I can't believe this," Fargo said incredulously. "He can't make a damn promise like that."

"Well, he did," Trudy said. "Go ask him yourself."

Fargo, disbelief still spinning inside him, scanned the figures from the other three Conestogas and saw mostly younger couples, steady, serious faces with tow-headed kids standing by, and felt the cold anger stabbing at him. This explained Oliver Kragg's equanimity. He knew his eager homesteaders were beyond listening after the major's assurances. He whirled, pulled himself onto the Ovaro, and swept the others with a frown. "I'll see you come morning," he bit out, and had the pinto in a fast canter as he threaded his way through the town to the stockade at the other end.

He rode into the inner court and reined to a halt in front of the major's quarters as the crisp, authoritative figure stepped outside.

"You seem in a hurry, Fargo," Major Thaxter observed.

"I've a lot of words wanting to be said," Fargo answered, and followed the major into the office. "I know about you and Strongarrow," he said, and Howard Thaxter's jaw tightened.

"You've been nosing around," Thaxter said thinly.

"You could say that," Fargo answered.

"It's no concern of yours, Fargo."

"Hell it isn't. You've got the Cheyenne all stirred up, and that's sure as hell my concern," Fargo snapped.

"The sooner I finish Strangarrow, the sooner things will quiet down, and I intend to do that very soon," the officer said.

"Maybe yes and maybe no," Fargo grunted.

"I'll have him soon."

"Meanwhile, how the hell can you give those Conestoga people assurances they'll be safe?" Fargo thrust at him angrily.

"Because they will be. I'll have at least two full platoons following behind them."

Fargo felt the furrow dig into this brow as he stared at the major. "Why? I don't get it," Fargo said. "Conscience?"

"Not at all," the major snapped.

"Since when does the army provide an escort service for wagon trains?" Fargo queried.

"It's my right, my decision. I'm field commander of this territory," Major Thaxter said authoritatively, and Fargo's thoughts swirled through his mind as he stared back at the man.

"You won't go all the way with them. You know it," Fargo said.

"Far enough," Thaxter said calmly, almost smugly.

Fargo's thoughts continued to swirl. It didn't hold together. Engaged in a vicious fight with the Cheyenne, Thaxter had no obligation—in fact, no right—to commit two full platoons to play shepherd for a wagon train. It made no sense tactically or strategically. It made no sense in a military way and it made no sense in any other way. Fargo pondered. Thaxter was a man of discipline, rules, regulations—a cold fish, not the kind of man given to generous gestures.

The major's cold voice broke into his thoughts. "Have you anything else to waste my time, Fargo?"

"Not for now," Fargo grated, and walked from the office.

Outside, night had fallen and he rode out of the stockade with a sourness inside him. Something was wrong. It just refused to add up right. He considered going to Ellie to spend the night, but he turned the thought down. It wouldn't be fair to her and he'd leave well enough alone. He sent the pinto out into the darkness until he found a small bower. After a supper of cold beef strips, he set out his bedroll, undressed, and stretched out, the Colt at his side. Not that he expected trouble. It was habit too much a part of him to change.

He lay still and listened to the soft night sounds as his thoughts traced idle patterns through his mind. It was useless to try to convince Kragg's homesteaders not to go, he reflected. They had the major's assurance, he grunted bitterly, and he had only words and warnings to counter that. But that assurance was a sham, a fraud, he was certain. But why had Major Howard Thaxter offered the assurance, or the escort? It still refused to add up right. There was something wrong, very wrong, and he finally went to sleep with the uneasiness inside him like an undigested meal.

When morning came and he woke, dressed, and turned the pinto into the hills, he again frowned at the fresh pony prints. Too many many, he grunted, small parties moving in different directions. Scouting parties, he noted, and in the distance he saw the spiral of dust in a straight line and the v-shaped company pennant came into view. He halted, watched the troopers ride on out of sight, and turned away with his jaw tight. The Cheyenne with their scouts, the major with his patrols, both sides probing, searching, ready for a quick strike but mostly maneuvering, preparing for a major battle.

Fargo continued to ride the hills and made plans of his own as he mentally marked out the trails that would take the heavy Conestogas through the base hills. But that would be only a start, of course, and when he finally finished, the sun was in the afternoon sky. He turned the Ovaro back down the low hills toward town, avoided a party of six Cheyenne warriors as they rode casually across the terrain, and hurried on to the relatively flat land below. When he reached Crooked Branch, the sun had begun to dip toward the horizon and he halted at the hotel to find only Elsa Cord there, a loose silk robe encasing her full figure.

"Oliver's picking up a few more supplies," the woman said. "You can say whatever it is to me."

"You're crazy, all of you, but it seems I made a deal and I'll keep my word," Fargo said. Elsa smiled as though she'd never had any doubts. "I'm going to try to convince all of you to turn back," he added.

"You won't be sorry you came."

"You keep saying that."

Her brown eyes danced with dark fire, and her arms came up and encircled his neck and her full lips pressed against his mouth, hungry pressure, pushing, working until she pulled away. "That convince you?" Elsa said.

"It'll help," Fargo said blandly.

"I'll tell Oliver you made your decision," she said. "Do we leave tomorrow?"

"Tell you, come morning. I've a friend to see before I go," Fargo answered, and turned to leave.

"Isn't there anything else you want to ask me?" Elsa said, a sly smile slipping across her wide-cheekboned face.

"When the time comes." Fargo laughed and hurried from the room.

The twilight had gone into darkness, and when he reached the wagons, a small fire burned for the supper meal. He saw Trudy among the others who looked up as he dismounted. "Haven't changed my mind about a damn thing. You're making a mistake, all of you, but we'll break trail within a day," he said, and heard the excited murmur that rose at once. He turned away, led the Ovaro from the wagons when he heard the quick footsteps hurrying after him.

"You could stay for supper," Trudy said.

"No, thanks," Fargo said grimly. "I can't watch people so happy to get themselves killed."

"It won't be that way. Didn't you speak to Major Thaxter?" she returned.

"I spoke to him. Haven't changed my mind any," Fargo said. "The major might just be a goddamn fool. That's the kindest thing I have to say about him."

"What do you mean by that?" Trudy frowned.

"I'm not sure, but something stinks," Fargo said, bitterness swirling through him. "And as for you, honey, you give me trouble and you're out."

"Why are you being this way? I haven't tried to do anything to you, certainly not on purpose," Trudy said, sounding genuinely hurt.

Fargo drew a deep sigh. "Knew a farmer once, tried to put a big Brahmin ox in a small box stall. It was a bad idea, and the ox flattened him against the stall as if he were a pancake. The ox didn't do it on purpose. He just got excited. But you know something. That farmer was just as dead as if the ox did it on purpose," Fargo said. "Good night, honey."

He walked on, heard her whirl and hurry back to the wagons. He led the pinto through town until he reached the saloon. He saw the palomino among the horses tethered at the hitching post. He tied the Ovaro alongside it and entered the smoky room. His eyes scanned the bar and found Canyon O'Grady at once. But then he was an easy man to spot, Fargo reminded himself. He pushed himself a place alongside the big, flame-haired man and saw that Canyon's usually roguish face held a tiredness he'd never seen in it before. "I'd say you've had no luck, friend," Fargo observed.

"And you'd be right, lad," Canyon said. "Nobody

in this saloon known him or anyone that fits his description. Maybe he didn't come this way, after all. Maybe my instincts have been wrong, a possibility that hurts even to contemplate." The big Irishman's crackling blue eyes searched Fargo's face. "You're a troubled man, too, Fargo," he said. "Not by your decision. You made that before we returned yesterday."

Fargo allowed a wry smile at Canyon's acute observation. "Something's been added," he said. "Something I can't figure." As Canyon listened, Fargo told him of his visit to the major and the man's assurances to the wagon train. "Something's wrong, dammit," Fargo added when he finished.

"It is dammed odd, to say the least," Canyon agreed. "But you can't complain about having a cavalry escort."

"I'll stop complaining when I start understanding," Fargo said. "What's your next move? Going on east?"

"No," Canyon O'Grady said, and slammed his fist onto the bar in a sudden explosion of frustration. "He's somewhere around here. I can feel it in my bones. My information told me he was heading to the Wind River Range, and that makes sense for him. To make it worse, he could be traveling with a woman, and that'd put another face on it."

Fargo held a long glance on the big red-haired man as he turned Canyon's words in his mind. It was probably just a coincidence, he mused, yet the words nagged at him. "You say he might be traveling with a woman?" Fargo queried.

"He could be. I'm not sure of that," Canyon answered.

"What's he look like, this feller you're chasing?"

"Medium height, thin, hairline going back, the nervous-looking kind with eyes that never stop darting back and forth like a damn ferret," Canyon said.

Fargo's lips pursed as he held Canyon O'Grady in a

sidelong stare. The odds of coincidence had just taken a precipitous drop. "Let's talk some more, but not here," he said, and started for the door as Canyon hurried after him.

Outside, the Trailsman climbed onto the Ovaro and rode in silence, Canyon a half-pace behind him. He rode from town, halted under the wide branches of a tanbark oak, and turned to face Canyon, who watched him with his snapping blue eyes narrowed.

"I might be able to help you find this hombre you're looking for," Fargo said. Canyon's eyes widened with curiosity. "If his name's Oliver Kragg," Fargo added, and saw curiosity give way to surprise. He chuckled and leaned against the tree. "Looks like I struck pay dirt, friend," he slid out.

"I didn't say that, lad." Canyon laughed, recovering with a quickness Fargo had to admire.

"That's the trouble, my friend, you don't really ever say anything. But I want that to stop. You level with me and I'll put you onto Oliver Kragg. No straight talk, no Kragg," Fargo said. "Your deal, friend."

Canyon thought for a long moment, his eyes taking in the measure of the big man who waited in front of him. Slowly, his charming, roguish smile slid over his face. "I guess there's a time when you have to trust somebody," O'Grady said. "You're a man to trust, Fargo, and God knows there are too few of them."

"Who the hell are you, O'Grady?" Fargo asked. "Let's start with that."

"I've told you about myself," Canyon said.

"I want to know the part you haven't told me," Fargo said, annoyance creeping into his voice. "No more wanderer, tinker, and odd-jobs bullshit."

Canyon O'Grady put his head back as he laughed. "It's not entirely a lie. I mean, there's a kind of truth in it, lad," he said. "I do odd jobs for the government, whatever they fancy suits my talents."

"For the government?" Fargo frowned.

Canyon rummaged deep into his saddlebag and finally brought out a small square of paper folded over once. He handed it to Fargo, who held it up to catch the moonlight as he peered at the words printed on it.

Be It Known to All That
Mr. Canyon O'Grady
Is an Agent of the United States Government.

By the Powers Invested in Me,
James Buchanan
President of these United States

Fargo handed the square of paper back to Canyon, who promptly pushed it down to the bottom of his saddlebag again. "Does that make you a federal marshal?" Fargo queried.

"Good Lord, no," Canyon said. "Federal marshal's wear badges and go about arresting people. Sometimes they're the law where there is no law but mostly they chase down those already wanted and with warrants out for them. A government agent is an investigator. I catch them in the act, not afterward. I could be sent anywhere to do anything."

"And you've been sent after Oliver Kragg," Fargo said.

"Yes, and now you can tell me what you know about him," Canyon said.

"He's organized the wagon train I'm breaking trail for," Fargo said, and Canyon O'Grady's brows lifted in surprise. "That's right, hired me for the job three months back. He has six Conestogas full of eager homesteaders ready to roll, and he's promised each family a thousand dollars when they reach Jackson Hole."

The surprise had turned to a frown on Canyon's face. "Tell me more. This is sure not what I expected," he said.

Fargo recounted the details of the wagon-train venture, from the basic concept of pioneering a new community to the pressures of time. When he finished, he watched Canyon continue to frown into the night. "I take it this doesn't fit the Oliver Kragg you're looking for," he commented.

"No, it sure doesn't, on the face of it, but then it might. I'm told he's a very clever customer, perhaps a lot more than anybody knows."

"Why has he a government agent on his tail?" Fargo said. "Namely, you."

"It seems that over a half-million dollars' worth of United States treasury bonds have disappeared from the office of the southwest region over the last ten years," Canyon said.

"That's a lot of bonds." Fargo whistled.

"Nobody noticed because they were taken in small bundles over the years. The loss was only discovered when there was a long-overdue audit about three or four months ago. These bonds are payable to the bearer. Whoever has them can cash them in anywhere. Now, the man who was in charge of that treasury office for the past ten years was . . ."

"Oliver Kragg," Fargo put in.

"Himself." Canyon nodded. "To add to the pot, Kragg up and left at the same time the bonds were discovered missing."

"I'd say that nails it down pretty good," Fargo remarked.

"Not good enough. Kragg sent a letter that claimed he knew nothing about the thefts, and right now we've no proof. A lot of suspicious things that point to him, but no proof. I was sent to find him and the bonds."

"How the hell does his organizing a wagon train fit in?"

"It could fit. For one thing, he'd need a wagon. That many bonds would take up a lot of space, much more than he could put on a packhorse. What better place to hide them and himself than to be part of a wagon train? It's plain he planned very carefully."

"It's still got holes. He doesn't have a wagon himself in the train. None of the Conestogas are his," Fargo said.

"You sure of that?"

"Positive."

"Maybe he's got the six Conestogas carrying the bonds. Maybe he's got them all in it without their knowing it," Canyon pondered aloud.

"They came and joined him in town so that doesn't seem likely, but then it's possible," Fargo said. "Let's go see what we can find out." He pulled himself onto the Ovaro and Canyon swung in alongside him. "I'll say you're an old friend I hired to ride guard with me," Fargo said, and Canyon nodded agreement. "You haven't told me where those bushwhackers on the ridge fit in?" Fargo said as they rode.

"I was in a tiny dot of a town, a saloon and a few buildings. I'd heard Kragg had been that way and I made the mistake of letting it be known that I'd money on me for the right information. They decided to follow and relieve me of the money," Canyon explained.

"Where does Elsa Cord fit in?" Fargo asked.

"Is she with him?"

"She is."

"We thought she might be, but we didn't know," Canyon said. "She was his assistant. He had to have her help him to file fake records and do all the paperwork needed to cover up the thefts each month."

Fargo nodded and thought about Elsa Cord's sensuousness and her hardly veiled promises. Maybe she'd been Kragg's helper but maybe she'd also be his weak spot. "Why would he risk his neck crossing Cheyenne country?" Fargo asked.

"He knows the government's looking for him. He can't risk trying to cash in the bonds anywhere nearby. He's got to get to Canada, where he'll be able to cash them in at his leisure. This is the quickest route north. Time's important to him, too."

Canyon fell silent and rode on until they reached the six Conestogas.

Clothes were still being hung out to dry overnight and Fargo saw Ben Deakens beside the tail of his wagon. Trudy stepped outside as the Trailsman pulled to a halt. "This is Canyon O'Grady, an old friend," Fargo introduced. "He's agreed to ride along to help me keep my scalp."

"Welcome aboard," Ben Deakens said, and received one of Canyon's wide, charming smiles that took in Trudy.

"Need some answers," Fargo said. "I need to know what's in every wagon. As wagon master, everybody gives you a list of what they're carrying."

"They're all carrying pretty much the same thing, same as we are," Deaken said. "Household goods, clothes, pots and pans, some furniture, maybe a cot or two. Everyone has a trunk or chest of personal things, bible, old pictures, family records. Most carry a few bags of coin and all a good supply of tools. That's about it."

"For each wagon?" Fargo pressed.

"For each wagon. Of course, those carrying two families would have two sets of most everything," Deaken said.

"Does Oliver Kragg have you carrying any trunks or boxes for him?" Fargo asked.

"No," Deakens said. "Not a one."

"He have anybody else carrying things for him," Fargo questioned.

"No, not at all," Ben said. "Besides, what with two families in most of the wagons there'd be no room for anybody else's extra baggage."

"You're sure?" Fargo pressed.

"Sure I'm sure," the man said with a trace of annoyance.

Fargo glanced at Canyon and caught his faint nod. "Thanks. Guess that's it, then," he said, and paused at Trudy's frowning glance. "You've something to say?" he tossed at her.

"I'm wondering if this is just careful attention to detail or something else," Trudy said stiffly.

"Such as?" Fargo snapped.

"Another excuse to try to get us to turn back," she returned. "It won't work."

"Wouldn't think of it, honey. We roll, come morning," Fargo said, and sent the Ovaro into a fast trot.

"She likes you, lad," Canyon said when he caught up to the pinto.

"She's a damn package of trouble," Fargo growled. "But not as much as we have. This just doesn't make any damn sense. If he's without the bonds, he could just be running to save his tail for now. Maybe he's stashed them someplace and figures to come back again when the pressure's off."

"It'd be a risk for him. Given a few months' time, we'll have word of stolen treasury bonds circulated to every bank. Cashing them in will become harder and riskier the longer he waits," Canyon said. "No, we're missing something here. Why did he plan all this? Why'd he put this whole, elaborate scheme in motion? Why the homesteader story and a thousand dollars promised to every family? Why'd he need all that?

Why didn't he just buy himself passage along with them?"

"Dammed if I can figure it. He has to have a reason," Fargo said. "Think you ought to say something to Major Thaxter?"

"With no proof at all?" Canyon returned. "Right now he's a man who's organized a wagon train and is helping a lot of eager homesteaders. We've no proof of anything else."

"He doesn't know you at all, does he?"

"No, we don't have to worry about that, come morning. You'll play your part and do what you were hired to do. I'll go along and we'll both see what happens. That's all we can do for now."

"You worry about Kragg and I'll worry about the major and his damn-fool assurances that don't make any sense, either," Fargo said. "Now let's get some shut-eye." He found a spot under a pair of red cedars and laid out his bedroll as Canyon O'Grady did the same nearby.

"Thanks for your help, lad," Canyon said.

"I feel better," Fargo murmured.

"For a good deed?"

"For knowing who the hell you are finally," Fargo returned, and heard the red-haired man's chuckle as he fell asleep.

8

Morning dawned with a bright sun. When Fargo rode into town, Canyon at his side, he noticed the activity in the stockade as he passed. The Conestogas were waiting when he reached them, Ben Deakens in the driver's seat of the lead wagon, Trudy beside him in a green-and-white-checked shirt that outlined the very high, very round breasts.

"We're all ready to go, Fargo," Deakens called out, and Fargo returned the friendly waves from the other wagons. His eyes scanned the wagons and returned to Ben Deakens.

"I don't see Kragg," he said.

"Expect him any minute," Deakens said.

Fargo saw four troopers ride toward him and come to a smart halt alongside the lead Conestoga.

"Trooper Devins, sir," the first soldier said to Deakens. "We'll be riding along with you."

"Just four of you?" Fargo frowned.

"The full platoons will be following at a distance," the trooper said, and took the other three men behind the last wagon.

Fargo was the first to see Elsa Cord approaching on a gray mare, the woman's wide-cheeked face severe. She drew to a halt before Ben Deakens but swept the other wagons with a glance.

"Oliver's taken sick. He won't be starting off with you. Neither will I, of course," she announced, and Fargo caught the quick glance Canyon threw at him.

"What's the matter with him?" Trudy asked, concern quick in her voice.

"It's a flare-up of his malaria. It comes on like this, all of a sudden. He runs a terrible fever until it passes," Elsa said. "But he wants you to start without us. There's been enough time lost already. When he's better in a few days, we'll catch up to you. We'll be able to follow the wagon tracks."

"Well, if you're sure that's what he wants," Ben said.

"That's exactly what he wants. You go on and we'll be catching up to you soon as Oliver's fever passes," Elsa said. "Good luck till then." She executed a wave that took in everyone, and turned the gray mare and started back to town.

Fargo moved to the forefront of the wagons and glanced down the line. "Let's roll," he called out, and brought the pinto to a walk in front of the first Conestoga, Canyon beside him.

"I don't like this," Canyon murmured. "Something doesn't smell right. All of a sudden he's not going along."

"What the hell does it mean?" Fargo muttered back.

"I don't know, but I don't like it," Canyon said.

"He goes to all this trouble, even if part of it's a lie, and then cancels out. That makes even less sense than before."

"That's why I don't like it. When we're a few miles out of town, you send me off someplace. I'll be going back to glue my eyeballs to that hotel."

"I'll keep the going slow so I can come back myself tonight. How'll I know you're still watching?" Fargo asked.

"I'll tie the palomino to the hotel hitching post. If

you don't see it, that means Kragg's gone and I've gone with him," Canyon said.

"Maybe he really is sick," Fargo said. "Why would he pull a fake sickness after all the trouble he's gone to to get these wagons rolling with himself a part of it?"

"I don't know, my friend, but I'm sure going to find out," Canyon muttered, and lapsed into silence as they passed the stockade.

Fargo glanced back when the last of the wagons rolled on and he saw no two platoons swinging from the stockade. But the four troopers seemed unconcerned and Fargo returned to leading the Conestogas forward. He was into the base of the range by afternoon and he sent Canyon off with a loud order to scout the terrain on all sides. He rode forward himself and scouted a broad passage that would easily accommodate the heavy Conestogas. But then he expected the passages at the base of the range to be broad and easy. Two trails of pony prints crossed his path, neither more than a day old but both small scouting parties, and he returned to Ben Deakens and paused for a moment.

"Stay on this passage. I'll be back soon," he said, and sent the pinto on past the other wagons to pause again beside the four troopers that brought up the rear of the line. "I don't see any sign of the major and his two platoons, soldier," he said.

"He's back there, sir," the trooper said.

"I'll have a look for myself just in case he had to change his plans," Fargo said with a generosity he didn't feel, and sent the pinto into a canter. He rode back over the terrain they had come, the wagon wheels easy to see in the dirt. His eyes swept the horizon for a sign of the platoons and found nothing, and after he'd ridden for some twenty minutes, he turned the horse around and headed back to the wagons.

Dusk was settling in when he reached them; he paused beside the troopers. "Something's wrong. I didn't see any sign of the major and his platoons."

"How far back did you go?" the soldier asked.

"About twenty minutes of good steady riding."

"You didn't go back far enough. He's stay a half-hour's ride back," the soldier said.

"A half-hour back?" Fargo frowned. "Why so far back?"

"He wants to be sure he's completely out of sight of any Cheyenne watching the wagons."

Fargo frowned at the trooper as thoughts swirled through his head. "I thought the whole idea was to give the wagon train protection, a show of force."

The trooper shrugged. "I wouldn't know about that, sir. I only know what he's doing and what his orders are."

"What orders?" Fargo barked as the thoughts inside him grew sharper.

"If there's an attack, we're to turn and race back to tell him," the soldier said. "Those are our orders."

"A half-hour's ride each way," Fargo thought aloud. "That means he wouldn't get back here with the platoons until an hour after the attack."

"I guess so, sir," the trooper said, and Fargo moved the Ovaro forward, the sharp thoughts inside him turning sour.

"Bastard," Fargo muttered aloud as he rode. "God-damn son of a bitch bastard."

One piece of the puzzle had suddenly fallen into place. Major Thaxter's bland assurance to the wagon train had taken on a new face, a self-serving, ugly face. Protection and safety really had another name. Fargo rode past the lead Conestoga, and as the dusk began to turn into dark, he found a cut on one side of the passage plenty large enough for the wagons to camp.

A small fire was lighted and the supper meal prepared. He had just adjusted the cinch strap on the Ovaro when Trudy appeared. "You're welcome to take supper with us," she said, and he took in her prettiness in the soft light.

"Some other time," he said. "I'm riding out right now."

"At night?" She frowned.

"Sometimes that's best for some kinds of scouting," Fargo said. "See you, come morning." He swung onto the horse and left her staring after him with a frown that held the edge of suspicion in it. He rode on up the passage a dozen yards, then veered into the trees and circled the wagons to emerge on the passage a dozen yards below. He put the horse into a fast canter that became a gallop, and once again he made a wide circle when he reached the spot where the major and his troopers had bedded down. He had plenty to say to the major but he'd decided to get back to town first. Maybe the other pieces of the puzzle would fall into place also. That would be best before facing Thaxter.

Fargo concentrated on riding and pushed further speculation away, and when he reached town, he reined up outside the hotel. He found the palomino at the hitching rail and that meant that Canyon was somewhere close, still watching and waiting for something to happen.

Fargo strode into the hotel and to Room Three. Elsa Cord opened the door at his knock and he saw the surprise flood her broad face.

"What are you doing here?" she gasped. "You're supposed to be in the mountains with the wagons."

"I was. I rode back to pay you a visit." Fargo smiled and stepped into the room. The door to the adjoining room was shut, he noted at once. "Mr. Kragg in there?"

"Yes," Elsa said. "When he's like this, he has to

stay in a dark room and just be left alone. There's nothing to be done for him except give him his medicine. For most of the time he's really in a kind of shivering coma."

"He's lucky to have you around," Fargo said.

"You didn't come back just to tell me that." Elsa drew the loose, blue silk robe tighter.

"No, I came back because I got to thinking that maybe he wouldn't recover fast and you'd never catch up to us," Fargo said. "This way I won't be disappointed."

The woman offered a slow smile. "You take a lot for granted."

"You made the promises, honey. You've been waving it in front of me ever since we met," Fargo said. "You saying you've changed your mind? I might have to camp here until you change it back."

"You won't have to do that. Just let me see to Oliver for a moment," Elsa said, and slipped into the adjoining room.

Fargo sat down and strained his ears but the door was solid and he picked up nothing. He was watching the door when it opened and Elsa returned to the room.

"He's in one of those deep sleeps that come over him at times like this," she said. "It'll last probably all night." She came toward him and the loose silk robe fell open just enough for him to glimpse heavy, creamy mounds that quickly vanished as she pulled the robe closed. She halted in front of him, the dark sensuousness swimming in her eyes. "You've surprised me, really, coming back like this," she said.

"Don't be surprised, be complimented," Fargo said, and she smiled as she embraced the thought.

"Yes, I like that," Elsa Cord said. She pulled the silk belt on the robe open and let the garment fall to the ground.

Fargo's eyes moved over a body that, for all its full-fleshed substance, still managed to exude an earthy, perhaps raw sexuality. Heavy, very white breasts were each topped by a brown-pink nipple on a light-brown areola; a layer of fat covered her abdomen beneath it and her stomach held its own convex curve that dropped down to a thickly tangled black nap. Her wide hips and strong legs still retained a shapeliness despite ten pounds extra they carried. Yet all of it balanced, broad shoulders and broad hips, the extra flesh on her adding to a carnality that reached out. She stepped to him, arms sliding around his shoulders, and her mouth found his, a hungry, eager pressure.

He responded as he pulled clothes off and she sank down on a small, hooked rug that covered the center of the floor. "Sorry the bed's in the other room," Elsa murmured as she rubbed her heavy breasts against his muscled chest.

He saw her stomach thrust forward, withdraw, and come forward again, and the sensuousness in her eyes had given way to a piercing hunger. "Hold the thought, honey," Fargo said as he rose and took hold of a straight-backed chair.

"What are you doing?" Elsa frowned as he crossed the room and wedged the top of the chair under the doorknob of the door to the adjoining room. "I told you Oliver was hard asleep."

"I know, but folks wake up suddenly." Fargo smiled.

"He won't," Elsa said.

"I don't like surprises," Fargo said as he crossed the room to her. She seemed flustered, unsure of herself for a moment. He halted before her and felt himself swelling as he stared down at her full-figured ripeness. Her eyes moved over him, lingering, and he heard the soft hiss of breath from her as she stared at him. "Jeeez," she murmured, and he dropped to his knees in front of her.

Elsa reached her hand out and curled her fingers around him, drew him to her breasts, and again he saw her stomach lift, push forward, and fall back again. She pulled at him, caressed his burgeoning warmth, fondled and stroked, threw herself against him, and pulled her face down to him, small moaning sounds coming from her.

"It's been a long time since you enjoyed it," Fargo murmured, and she nodded frantically as she almost devoured him as a starving person devours food. She fell back on the rug, pulled him with her, and he heard her deep groaning sound as his strength fell against the tangled black nap. Her full thighs fell open and she pushed herself upward as she groaned again from deep inside. Her arms around his neck pulled his face down into the heavy, white mounds. He turned so he could take one large brown-pink nipple in his mouth, then the other. "Aaaah, ah, ah, yes, Jeeez, yes," Elsa groaned as her full thighs pressed themselves around his waist and she groaned and grunted as she heaved under him.

"Take me, God, take me, big man," Elsa breathed. She lifted herself again under him, her dark, wet portal opening wide, the flesh imploring, echoing her words. Her arms were clutching him tight. He moved, let himself find her wanting lips and thrust forward.

Elsa uttered a growling groan, an animallike sound that quickly became a series of gasping, grunting noises as she pushed and heaved with him, transformed into an explosion of pure sexual energy. Elsa carried no delicate ecstasy in her, no warm and quivering sensitivity. The woman was all simple carnality, absolute erotic hunger that allowed no room for anything but unvarnished passion. Her growling groans and deep-throated gasps held their own excitement, and Fargo felt himself being carried along with her, pushing and thrusting with a kind of savage pleasure.

Grateful for the full-fleshed cushion of her body, he pressed harder as she growled, clutched at him, and gasped for more until suddenly he felt her begin to shake, her thighs around him slapping against his hips. The sound that rose from deep inside Elsa was a half-growl, half-scream, a low and rolling sound, guttural in its absolute deep pleasure, and Fargo saw her eyes had become half-glazed and staring.

"Aaaagggggggrrrroooooow," the woman roared as her moment came, sweeping through her as her belly moved in and out with deep, gasping breaths. "Jeeeez, jeeez, oh, oh my God," she finally managed as her heaving, gasping form gave its final quaking shudder and she lay still, arms still around Fargo's neck, thighs still against his ribs.

As he watched, her eyes slowly lost their glazed stare and her arms fell away. She lay quietly heaving and her legs straightened, fell limply down beside him, and another groan came from her as he slid from her. Her eyes returned to normal and she half-turned on her side, her heavy breasts falling down to touch the rug.

"I'd say this ended a long dry spell," Fargo ventured and drew a wry smile from the woman that was its own admission.

She reached out and drew the silk robe around her shoulders as she watched him dress. "Too bad you can't stay," she said.

"Think about next time."

"Next time?" she echoed, a fleeting frown touching her brow.

Fargo's thoughts snapped inside him. "Yes, after you and Kragg catch up to the wagons."

"Oh, yes, of course," the woman quickly said, and Fargo smiled inwardly. She had slipped for an instant and her moment's lapse meant only one thing: She and Kragg had no intention of rejoining the Conestogas.

It was time for a meeting with Canyon O'Grady, Fargo decided. He finished dressing as Elsa walked to the door with him.

"See you soon?" Fargo said.

"Soon." The woman nodded, and he walked from the room but not before he caught the moment of reluctance in her eyes. Elsa had enjoyed every second of their lovemaking—there was no question of that, Fargo knew—but it had been part of something else. He hurried away with his lips turned grim.

Outside, he halted, stared at where the palomino had been hitched. The horse was gone, and that meant two things: Kragg had left and Canyon had gone after him.

Fargo heard the grim snort that escaped his lips. Elsa had given Kragg time to flee while she made love, and now it was plain that the entire story about his attack of malaria had been nothing but a fake.

The Trailsman walked around to the far side of the hotel and found the open window through which Kragg had fled. He stared at the dark empty square for a moment and then sauntered back to the hotel entrance. He'd never pick up Canyon's trail in the inky dark of the night, but another visit to Elsa Cord might bring some answers. It was worth a try, he decided, and the woman's eyes widened with astonishment again when she opened the door.

"Fargo. So soon? You're full of surprises tonight," she said.

"That makes two of us," Fargo said, and strode into the room. She had taken the chair from where he'd wedged it under the doorknob. "Good," he said. "My mistake. It was never needed." With a quick, sudden motion, he raised his leg and kicked the door open and saw Elsa draw breath in sharply. "Nobody there. Another surprise," Fargo bit out, and whirled on the woman. "I want some answers from you," he growled.

"He was there. He suddenly felt better and went out for some air while you were gone," Elsa said, swallowing hard.

"Is that the best you can do, Elsa?" Fargo snorted.

"I don't know what you mean," the woman said, trying to sound arrogant.

"I know about Oliver and you and the treasury bonds," Fargo said, and saw the instant flash of surprise in her eyes. She snuffed it out at once and her face tightened.

"What are you talking about?"

"You know damn well. I want to know why this goddamn wagon train. Why all this scheme to offer a thousand dollars to each family that gets to Jackson Hole? Why hire me on to break trail?"

"It was all explained to you. There's nothing else."

"Hell there isn't," Fargo snapped, and his hand shot out, seized the robe at the neck, and yanked Elsa Cord toward him. "How does it all fit together, dammit?" he roared. "The Conestogas, the stolen treasury bonds, all of it?"

"I don't know what you're talking about. Let go of me," she said, and Fargo swore inwardly. She'd been around too long and was too hard inside to fold easily. He took his hand from the robe and stepped back.

"You're being real dumb. Talk, and maybe you can avoid a noose."

"You've gone mad, it seems," Elsa said adamantly. "Oliver made a mistake in hiring you."

"More than he knows," Fargo grunted. "I'm going to get the answers to this damn thing."

"You going to wait here?" the woman asked with seeming unconcern.

"No, there's a wagon train that's going to need all the help it can get. But I'll be back this way when I'm ready." Fargo yanked the door open and strode from the room and out into the night. He pulled himself onto the Ovaro and set the horse into a gallop. He slowed after he reached the base of the hills and brought the horses into a steady but ground-consuming pace. He went over everything that he'd learned as he rode, including all that Canyon O'Grady had told him, and he still couldn't fit the pieces together.

Finally one thought came to rest in his mind:

Canyon had said they'd no actual proof Kragg had taken the bonds. Everything pointed to him, but he had denied it. What if he were telling the truth? Fargo mused. Then the wagon train would be a legitimate venture on its own with no pieces to fit together. But that still didn't explain why Kragg was seemingly ducking out on the venture he'd gone to such trouble to put together. Fargo grimaced and snapped off thoughts as he came to where Major Thaxter's platoons were camped, and he again made a wide circle and rode on. He still didn't want to accept the dark thoughts that had spiraled through him to explain the major's actions. He'd give the man another day, he decided. Maybe he intended moving in closer when the wagons went deeper into the range.

Shaking away the dark cloud of suspicions, Fargo hurried on and finally reached the spot where he'd left the six Conestogas, their tall, rounded shapes silhouetted in the last of the moonlight. He dismounted, set out his bedroll, and drew sleep around himself at once. He'd have three or four hours at best, he knew, and let the night sounds fade away.

When morning came and he woke, he saw that some of the wagons were up and ready to roll. The sun was full over the high crags: he'd slept an hour longer than he'd intended. He washed and dressed hurriedly, gratefully accepted a tin mug of coffee from

Cy Estes, and when he finished, he saddled the Ovaro and found Trudy beside him.

"Where's your friend?" she asked. "Still out scouting?"

"You've got it, honey," Fargo said, and saw the faint smile in her eyes.

"Why don't I believe you?" she asked.

"Maybe because you've a suspicious mind," he said. "Get to your wagon. We're rolling out."

She left with just the touch of a flounce, yellow shirt setting off the black of her hair, the very high, round breasts bouncing.

Fargo climbed into the saddle and waved the Conestogas forward. The four troopers fell in at the rear, he noted, and he pulled alongside Ben Deakens. Trudy immediately poked her head out from inside the canvas top of the wagon. "Stay on this passage, follow it up, and I'll meet you later," he said, and rode forward at once.

He took the passage long enough to see that it remained passable and then cut into the thick stands of box elder and hawthorn that covered the low hills, his eyes sweeping the ground. Once again he saw the Indian pony prints that crossed and recrossed the woodlands, all only day or two old. When he finally returned to the top of the passage, he scanned the high ridges but saw no bronzed horsemen. He grunted, a grim sound. They were there, he knew, watching, waiting, and he sent the pinto forward through the passage as it narrowed for a few hundred yards and the trees grew almost across the path.

He emerged suddenly and saw the high plateau spreading out in front of him and wrestled with the mixed emotions that stabbed at him. The terrain was perfect for the heavy Conestogas, flat and grassy, and it stretched out deep into the mountains. It would cut days off climbing mountain roads and save time and wear on horses and travelers. It was also perfect for the Cheyenne to sweep across in a full attack. They could explore out of the thick tree cover on either side of the high plateau and be in a full gallop instantly. But it would also give Thaxter's platoons a chance to make good time coming to the defense of the wagons.

Fargo turned the Ovaro around and knew the options were really so much empty conjecture. Ben Deakens and the others would insist on taking the opportunity to save time the high plateau offered.

Fargo rode back and into the passage until it narrowed. He drew to a halt and peered down as he watched the Conestogas come into sight, slowly rolling upward. His gaze went past the four troopers at the rear and he continued to peer beyond the wagons as they finally came up to where he waited. There was no sign of Major Thaxter and his men and Fargo cursed silently. Dark, sour thoughts rushed over him again and he knew it was becoming increasingly difficult to turn away from their bitter message.

He waved the wagons on, turned, and rode ahead of them and onto the plateau, where he waited as the afternoon sun began to slide over the high crags. He saw the excitement on their faces as the travelers saw the long stretch of flatland ahead of them. He turned away, rode on until the day began to slide into dusk.

He edged the wagons away from the center of the plateau and had them make a circle to one side as they halted for the night. Again, he squinted through the fading light but saw no sign of the major and his troopers. His mouth turned into a thin line and he swore silently and brought the Ovaro into the circle. He dismounted and watched as the Wilsons and Reicherts invited the four troopers to take the meal with them. He sat down between two of the wagons after he'd warmed his beef strips and watched the velvet blue of the night sky overhead.

He stayed seated as he saw the figure approaching him, yellow blouse a pale brightness under the moon that had taken the sky. "You don't have to stay off by yourself," Trudy said. "Or is this always the way with you?"

"Not always but mostly," Fargo said. "Especially when I'm thinking about how to say something I don't like saying and you won't like hearing."

"Maybe that's a good reason it shouldn't be said," Trudy returned airily.

"Maybe that's the best reason it should be said."

She made an annoyed face. "I guess we just see things differently."

"No," Fargo said. "One of us sees and the other doesn't."

"Good night," Trudy snapped. She whirled and strode away.

Fargo watched her reach her wagon in the last glow of the fire. He leaned back against one of the wagon shafts. Another night would make little difference, he realized, and maybe Canyon would show up with something to help. Fargo stretched out, the churning inside him made of frustration and bitterness, and he closed his eyes as the camp grew silent. But he could do no more than catnap, and the night had grown deep when he sat up as his ears picked up the sound of the horse approaching.

Fargo drew the Colt while he peered into the dark and saw the silhouette of the horse and rider materialize out of the night. He rose to his feet as the moonlight picked up the coppery sheen of the horse and stepped forward.

Canyon O'Grady spotted him at once, steered the palomino toward him, and swung to the ground before the horse halted. "Maybe you better sit down again, lad," he said.

9

"I've got the pieces and they're all rotten," Canyon said, folding himself to sit down by the wagon shafts.

"I've got some pretty damn rotten ones, too," Fargo snorted. "But you first."

"Kragg left the hotel by the window, but I suppose you know that now," Canyon began, and Fargo nodded. "I followed him, trailed him to a hideaway about fifteen miles west of here. He had a wagon there, a big California rack bed covered with tightly wrapped canvas. He had six gunhands with it. The bonds are in that wagon, you can bet on that."

Fargo frowned at the big, red-haired man. "I still don't put it together. Then why the wagon train?"

"That's what I wondered, too. I waited through the morning and watched them leave. They headed straight up the range, due north, just the way the Conestogas are going. They're almost paralleling the path you're taking with the wagon train. Only instead of Jackson Hole, he's heading for Canada."

"Right through the Cheyenne country." Fargo frowned.

"Exactly. It's the shortest route, and as I told you, time is important to him," Canyon went on. "But he knew the chances of getting through Cheyenne country alive were damn slim. He wanted to make sure he made it."

Fargo's thoughts were leapfrogging. "He set up the

whole thing," he said in awe. "The story about a man waiting to start a community, the thousand-dollar offer for each family, even hiring me, all to make sure it seemed real."

"And excite the settlers into going ahead with it," Canyon said.

"When all the while he was setting the wagon train up as a decoy. The Cheyenne will attack the Conestogas, have themselves another massacre, and while they're doing it, he'll slip through with his wagon."

"Bull's-eye," Canyon said. "Between the attack and dividing up the spoils later, he figures the Cheyenne will be busy and satisfied for a few days at least, long enough for him to get through the main part of the range and on his way safe and alive. The entire wagon train is a decoy, all planned to draw the Cheyenne to it while he slips past. No doubt Elsa was to have left the hotel with him, but your visit stopped that, so he went on his way alone. I'm sure they've arranged for her to meet up with him someplace."

Canyon halted and his lips drew back with anger. "He's sending all those people to their deaths to get away with his damn bonds. Now, that's a real rotten bastard," he finished.

"He's not alone," Fargo said, and watched O'Grady's eyes widen. "That bastard Thaxter's using them as bait. He gave them assurances that they'd be safe so they'd be sure to go on. But he's staying back so far it'll take him near an hour to reach the wagons when they're attacked. You know what that means?" Fargo asked rhetorically, and Canyon waited. "It means he's planned to hit the Cheyenne while they're busy attacking and burning the wagon train. He'll catch them by surprise and wipe them out."

Canyon's lips pursed. "Chances are it'll work. It's

an old tactical maneuver: strike your enemy when he's engaged in another battle."

"I'm sure it'll work but it'll be too late to save most of those in the wagon train. He's sacrificing them to get Strongarrow, it's as simple as that," Fargo said.

"And that makes him no better than Kragg."

"It makes him worse. I can understand Kragg. He's a thief out for himself. He's ruled by greed. He doesn't give a damn about anybody else," Fargo said. "But Thaxter's supposed to be an officer of the United States cavalry. He's here to protect people, not to use them as pawns."

"Kragg's ruled by greed. Thaxter's ruled by hate. The result's the same," Canyon said. "Men with their souls twisted out of shape."

"What now?" Fargo grunted.

"I'd say we tell your people in the morning," Canyon said. "Meanwhile, I need some sleep, and this seems as good a place as any." He stretched his big frame out on the other side of the wagon shafts and was asleep in minutes.

Fargo continued to stare into the night. A terrible certainty curled inside him. It wouldn't end so easily, by talk, by reasonable words and good advice. He lay back, closed his eyes, and let sleep come to him. There was nothing else to do now but wait.

When morning came he waited till everyone had had coffee and the horses were hitched to the wagons before he called them into a circle, Ben Deakens in the foreground, Trudy beside him, and he noted the amusedly tolerant half-smile on her lips.

"Got something to tell you," he began. "It's not going to make you happy. You've all been tricked, hornswoggled, and used. Oliver Kragg isn't coming to join you. Everything he told you was a lie." He paused and heard the half-gasp that rose, and his eyes swept the faces that now stared at him with frowns on each brow. "There's no thousand dollars waiting for each of you. That whole story was a lie," Fargo went on. "It was part of his plan to make sure you'd go through the Wind River Mountains. The man's a thief and a liar."

"Why would he do that?" Ben Deakens asked, and a murmur of assent rose from the others.

"He's set you up as decoy for the Cheyenne. While they're busy attacking you, he's going to slip through with a wagonload of stolen treasury bonds," Fargo said, and scanned the stony faces in front of him. "Ask Canyon O'Grady here. He saw Kragg with his wagon. That bout of sickness was phony, too."

"Mr. O'Grady's a friend of yours. He'll say whatever you want him to say," Trudy put in, and Fargo exchanged a glance of exasperation with Canyon. "I know you're convinced we should all turn back, Fargo. We all know that, but this is going a little far," she added.

"It's the dammed truth," Fargo snapped, and saw the others send uneasy glances among themselves.

Ben Deakens spoke for everyone there. "I'm afraid we feel pretty much like Trudy, Fargo. We just don't believe it. But even if we did, we're safe. Major Thaxter's following behind with his troops."

Fargo grimaced and drew a deep breath and there was weariness in his voice when he answered. "The major's using you, too," he said. "He wants the Cheyenne to attack you so he can come up and take them by surprise. He's staying so far behind that there's no chance they'll see him. He wants to make sure they'll attack you. Dammit, Kragg's using you as a decoy and Thaxter's using you as bait. You're not a wagon train. You're targets in the shape of Conestogas."

He saw the shock in their faces, and once again they

exchanged uneasy glances. They turned in a tight circle and murmured among themselves.

"I don't think they're believing you," Canyon muttered. "Especially about the major."

"I can't blame them. I've trouble believing it myself," Fargo grunted grimly, and saw Ben Deakens turn to him as the murmured conference ended.

"Maybe you think you're doing right by us with these stories, Fargo, and we can't be angry at you for that," Deakens said. "But we just can't find it in us to believe them. And it's no matter, anyway. If we did believe you, we'd still go on. There's good land for the taking at Jackson Hole and that's what we want, with or without the thousand dollars. If the Cheyenne attack, we'll just have to hold out till the major and his men get to us."

"Which means we feel you've an obligation to continue to break trail for us," Trudy added stiffly, and Fargo met her eyes. He pushed aside a half-dozen answers that rose up inside him and allowed a wry smile to touch his lips.

"Never said I wouldn't," he answered. "Roll your wagons." He swung onto the Ovaro and rode forward with Canyon alongside him, quickly moving ahead of the Conestogas. He set out across the high plateau, his lake-blue eyes sweeping the distant trees that bordered the flatland.

"You're thinking they deserve better," Canyon said.

"Yes, they've been taken all around."

"Not much you can do about that."

"Maybe I can still turn it around."

"How?"

"I'm going to pay Thaxter a visit. Maybe I can get him to remember who he is," Fargo said. "If I can get him to move up where the Cheyenne will see him, it's not likely they'll attack two full platoons."

"It's worth a try, though I'd not bet on your chances," Canyon said.

"I'll wait till most of the day's over. They'll let us go deep into the plateau, which means they won't hit us till tomorrow at best," Fargo said. "What are you going to do about Kragg?"

"I thought we might work that out," Canyon said blandly.

"We?"

"I'll help you and you help me," the Irishman said. "I'll stay on to help you. You'll be needing every bit of help you can get."

"That's for sure," Fargo agreed.

"Afterward, you help me go after Kragg. He's got six gunslingers riding herd on his wagon, seven if we count him. I know pretty much where he'll be by then and it won't be hard to pick up his tracks. But I'll need help. A bargain, lad?" Canyon said.

"A bargain," Fargo said. "You're a good man, Canyon O'Grady."

"I'm a gamblin' man. I'm gambling we'll both be around to go after Kragg," Canyon said, and Fargo's snort was a grim sound as his eyes swept the long high plateau. "You see anything I don't?" O'Grady asked.

"Not yet, but you can bet they see us," Fargo said. "They'll let us go deep into the plateau before they move on us. That means at least one more night without trouble." Fargo glanced back at the distant wagons.

By noon the sun had grown burning hot. Fargo let the wagons catch up and ordered a halt to water the horses from the extra water kegs each Conestoga carried.

Trudy paused beside him when they prepared to move on again. "You surprised me. I expected you'd protest more about staying on with us."

"My good deed for the month," Fargo said.

"I couldn't bring myself to believe you."

"You will," Fargo said. "I just hope you'll be alive to be sorry."

She studied him and he saw the edge of apprehension come into her eyes before she turned away and hurried to the wagon.

He turned and moved the pinto on across the plateau and concentrated on the trees again. But he saw no sign of any bronzed horsemen, the landscape still and peaceful, and he kept the Conestogas moving slowly under the hot sun. When dusk began to turn the day into soft lavender, he called a halt and paused beside Trudy and her uncle.

"Camp here," he said. "In a circle."

Trudy, again quick to pick up on the unsaid, frowned back. "You're riding out again," she said.

"Maybe," he said, and walked to the side with Canyon.

"She's right, isn't she, lad?" Canyon murmured.

Fargo nodded. "I'm going to pay Thaxter a visit. If I can reach him, maybe we can make it a clean sweep."

"I'm listening," Canyon said.

"I'm going to try to get Thaxter to move his troops up and do what he's supposed to do. If I can do that, Strongarrow may not risk an attack on two full platoons. In that case, he'll back off, but he'll be mad as hell. It's a sure thing he'll have his scouts charging all over the mountains, looking for something to attack."

"And they'll sure find Kragg and his wagon. Two birds with one stone," Canyon almost chortled. "I like it, lad, except for one thing." Fargo frowned and waited. "I don't see Thaxter going along with you."

"I've got to give it a try," Fargo said. "Their lives depend on it, whether they know it or not." He walked back to the wagons where Trudy still waited. "If I'm delayed getting back, Canyon will take you on," he told her.

"Where are you going?" Trudy asked.

"You concerned?" he asked blandly.

"What if I said yes?" she murmured almost crossly.

"I'd be grateful," Fargo said.

She made no reply and turned back to the circle of wagons.

"You better damn well get back," Canyon hissed into his ear. "I'm no trailsman."

"I'll be careful." Fargo laughed as he swung onto the pinto. He put the horse into a gallop as the dusk began to turn to grayness.

He rode hard and dusk had almost given way to dark when he reached the spot where the major had encamped for the night. He slowed and walked the horse forward. A sentry raised his carbine. "Come to see Major Thaxter," Fargo called out as more troopers hurried up, rifles at ready.

They motioned him forward and three of the soldiers escorted him to the small field then where he halted as Major Thaxter emerged.

"Man wants to see you, sir," one of the troopers said, and Fargo met the faint surprise in the officer's contained, intense face.

"Aren't you supposed to be with those Conestogas, Fargo?" the man asked.

"I'll be going back after I say my piece to you," Fargo said, and slid from the Ovaro.

Major Thaxter's eyes narrowed as he studied the big man with the grimly handsome countenance. "Come inside," Thaxter said, and led the way into the field tent, which was barely high enough for Fargo to stand up straight.

"I know what you're doing," Fargo said as the major turned to face him.

Thaxter offered a smile of amused tolerance. "I'm doing exactly what I promised I'd do for them, seeing to their safety," he said.

"Steershit," Fargo barked. "You've set them up as bait to lure Strongarrow out. They'll be wiped out by the time to get to them, but you'll hit the Cheyenne by surprise."

Thaxter's smile of amused tolerance vanished from his face as his eyes grew hard. "That Cheyenne is the root of all the trouble in this territory. It's my job to get rid of him, and that's what I'm going to do," he flung back.

"By sacrificing a whole wagon train of people," Fargo said.

"I'm doing no more than if I sent a detail of my troops to lure the Cheyenne out," the major said. "That's just good military tactics, and you wouldn't be saying a word then."

"That's right, because your troopers are paid to do their job. They're under your command, for good or bad. But this is a wagon train of settlers," Fargo said.

Major Thaxter's lips curled in disdain. "I'm making them part of a military operation. I've the authority to commandeer any civilian I want in this territory."

"You don't have the authority to lie, to sacrifice people. You commandeer, you tell why," Fargo returned. "I'll make a deal with you, Thaxter. You do what you promised those people you were going to do, protect them not use them. You bring your men up to those wagons right now or I'll report you to Washington and to general headquarters. I'll nail you down for what you are, a self-centered, glory-grabbing bastard who sent six wagons full of men, women, and children to their deaths to get at the Cheyenne."

"What makes you think they'd believe you, Fargo?" the major questioned thinly.

"Because I've a reputation for telling the truth, and the top command knows it," Fargo shot back. "You've got your choice, Major. You get your troopers up there to protect those Conestogas and find some other way up there to get at Strongarrow or I'll see you in front of a court-martial. You've five minutes to decide."

Thaxter's eyes were narrowed to slits of cold fury. "Wait outside," he murmured.

Fargo strode from the tent. He stepped a dozen paces away and saw the major bark orders to the corporal outside the tent.

"Get me Lieutenant Bond and Sergeant Murphy," Thaxter said, and the soldier hurried away.

Fargo stayed where he was as the two troopers appeared and went into the tent. They reappeared perhaps two minutes later and Fargo turned as the lieutenant and the sergeant approached him. The sergeant pulled an Army Colt from his holster and the lieutenant followed with his own sidearm.

"You're under arrest, mister," the lieutenant said. "I'll take that gun," he added, and pulled the Colt from Fargo's holster while the sergeant's revolver stayed trained on his prisoner.

"Put him in irons," he heard Thaxter's voice cut in, and turned to see the major at the entrance to the field tent. "I want a sentry on him through the night."

Fargo felt the iron manacles on his wrists almost instantly and he was led to the edge of the encampment.

"Sit down," the lieutenant ordered. Fargo obeyed and watched his ankles bound together with a length of rope. "You take first watch, Sergeant," the lieutenant ordered, and hurried away. Fargo's eyes peered at the sergeant and saw an experienced cavalryman, not the kind of man that could be easily tricked into a mistake and he cursed inwardly.

Night had blanketed the high plateau and the camp

became a silent, sleeping place within the hour. Fargo pressed his wrists hard against the manacles but realized they were fastened beyond prying open, and the sergeant watched from a half-dozen feet away with tolerant impassiveness. Fargo let his arms relax and his gaze roamed the perimeter of the camp. Thaxter had four sentries on duty, he saw, one facing in each direction. The sergeant's concern was strictly to watch him, Fargo realized as his mind raced to try to find a way to escape.

Another hour passed and he hadn't found a way yet when he saw the trim figure approaching from inside the camp.

"Take a five-minute break, Sergeant," Major Thaxter said, and the sergeant strolled away.

Fargo gazed up at the major's smug face. "You're only making it worse for yourself, Thaxter," he said.

"You won't be telling anyone anything, Fargo," the major said, contempt in his voice. "You'll simply be the victim of a stray bullet when the fighting starts."

"Bastard," Fargo hissed while he realized how easily the major could put words into action.

"Somebody might just stay alive in those Conestogas and talk about how you promised them protection," Fargo threw back, though he knew the threat was all emptiness.

The major's disdainful, icy smile said that he knew it also, and he turned away as the sergeant returned. "Watch him," he said to the soldier. "He's your only responsibility till you're relieved."

"Yes, sir," the sergeant said, and stepped another few feet from his prisoner. He fastened his eyes on the manacled figure on the ground and Fargo rolled onto his side with a silent curse.

He lay on his side as the night grew long and a half-moon rose high in the blue-black sky. The four sentries were silent, thin silhouettes around the perimeter of the camp, and Fargo closed his eyes and catnapped. He snapped awake every fifteen or so minutes and thoughts of how to escape had become only exercises in frustration. He watched the moon slowly begin its long glide across the sky and he rolled onto his back and saw the sergeant quickly peer hard at him.

"Relax, soldier," Fargo muttered, and returned to lie on his side after a few moments. He lay motionless and saw the sergeant step back a pace but continue his watch on him. Fargo lay still and knew the feeling of helplessness as the moon continued to move closer to the horizon, where dawn waited to bring the day.

He dozed again, perhaps another half-hour, then he woke with a tingling along the back of his neck. He lay motionless and felt his skin crawling, the hairs on his hands growing stiff. He knew the meaning of it, that inner consciousness sending its alarms, the thing some people called a sixth sense, others simply an unusual sensitivity given to but a few. But something was near on the dark plateau, Fargo knew, and without moving, he let his gaze sweep the limited area he could take in, but he saw nothing.

He stayed unmoving, hardly daring to breathe, and felt the presence near. He let his nostrils flare and tried to pick up the scent of Indian but failed. Deciding to turn on his back, he moved and immediately drew a moment of attention from the sergeant. He stayed on his back and turned his head sideways to scan the ground past where the trooper stood over him. One of the sentries in the distance became a thin black shadow, and he was about to turn on his side again when he spotted the flattened shape on the ground. Fargo stayed motionless, stared, and saw the shape move, inching its way along the grass. He couldn't discern anything more than the flattened shape, and he drew the air in through his nostrils again in a deep breath. But he detected no odor of fish oil or bear grease and he decided against alerting the sergeant.

He turned on his side again, facing the dark shape this time, and saw it move again, inch closer, and suddenly he glimpsed the shape take on a moment of definition, become a flash of full, tousled hair that he recognized even without the color.

He turned on his back again and began to pound his manacled wrists on the ground behind his back.

"What the hell are you doing?" the sergeant said, and took a step closer.

"Trying to get loose," Fargo snapped, and continued to pound his wrists against the ground as best he could.

"You can't get loose." The sergeant frowned. "And even if you could, I'm right here watching you."

Fargo saw the shape had stopped inching forward and risen up, taking on the unmistakable form of Canyon O'Grady. "I don't care. I'm going to try to get loose," Fargo said. Again he began to pound his wrists on the ground.

The sergeant, all his concentration on Fargo, took another step forward. "You crazy or something?" he said. "Cut it out."

"Go to hell," Fargo said, still holding the man's full attention as he saw Canyon running now on silent steps.

The sergeant continued to frown at him, uncertain of just what he should do. "Stop that, dammit," he finally blurted out just as Canyon O'Grady's big form rose up behind him and the butt of the heavy Army Colt crashed down on his skull, a dull thud. The sergeant collapsed into O'Grady's arms and the big man lowered him gently to the ground.

"We'll talk later," Canyon said as he knelt and untied the ropes binding Fargo's ankles. "Start crawling. The sentries are still on the watch."

Fargo stayed prone, pushed himself along the ground with his feet as he followed Canyon's crawling form. He'd gone only a few dozen yards, he realized, but it felt as though he'd gone a mile. He was able to use only the lower part of his body, and crawling became an even more awkward motion than usual. After they'd gone another twenty-five yards or so, Canyon halted and waited for Fargo to crawl up to him.

"I hope to hell you've some horses around here," Fargo muttered.

"Another fifty yards or so," Canyon said. "We're too close yet to do anything about those manacles."

"I know. Let's move on," Fargo said, and again began the awkward crawling motion, pushing into the ground with his legs and feet. But finally he saw the dark silhouette of three horses, and Canyon pushed upward and helped Fargo to his feet.

"We're far enough to walk the rest of the way now," he said.

"Why the three horses?" Fargo asked, and the big red-haired man didn't answer. But the question found its answer when Fargo saw the slender form come into sight when he reached the horses. "What's she doing here?" he asked Canyon.

"She saw me getting ready to ride out and asked where I was going. I decided it might be the best thing to let her see for herself. It's hard to keep disbelieving when you see with your own eyes," Canyon said. "When you didn't come back, I figured Thaxter had done something like this."

"I was to be the victim of a stray bullet after the righting started," Fargo said, and saw Trudy's grave face as she watched and listened.

"Hold still," Canyon said as he took a towel from his saddlebag, wrapped it around the manacles, and then pressed his revolver against the center of the irons. He fired and the towel dulled the sound as Fargo felt the manacles come loose. He pulled his hands free and quickly began to rub circulation back into his wrists. His eyes went to Trudy again and then back to Canyon. "I guess bringing her was the right thing," he said. "But I'm going back to get my Ovaro. I'll pick up my gun some other time."

"You know where the horse is?" Canyon asked.

"Tied with the army mounts," Fargo said. "I'll sneak around the other side."

"They've a sentry on each side," Canyon reminded him.

"Give me ten minutes, then you two charge from here. Yell, give out with war whoops, race back and forth, but stay just out of range and sight," Fargo said. "They'll switch to face your direction."

"A diversion. Got it." Canyon nodded.

Fargo went off at a fast trot. He made a wide circle and came at the camp from the far side, dropped to his stomach as he drew closer, and began to crawl the rest of the way. He was within ten yards of the dark figure of the sentry when he heard the night explode with sound, gunfire and war whoops. The camp erupted as troopers sprang to their feet. The sentry facing him ran to the other side with the others, and Fargo rose to one knee, waited, and saw Thaxter run from his field tent while donning his jacket.

Canyon and Trudy continued to raise a ruckus and Fargo hesitated, decided, and ran for the field tent. He ducked under the bottom flap and swept the interior, which was lighted by a low-burning candle. He spotted his Colt on the ground near a cot, scooped it up, and crawled back under the bottom edge of the tent.

The troopers were still peering into the night at the other side of the camp, and Fargo ran to where the horses were tethered in double rows, the Ovaro easy to spot among the brown Morgan army mounts. He untied the pinto, swung onto the horse, and raced away. He glanced back to see some of the troopers turn at the sound of hoofbeats at their backs, but he was already out of sight in the darkness. He raced in a wide circle until he spotted Canyon and Trudy. They had halted and he called to them and saw them turn to hurry after him.

"You did fine," he said when they caught up to him. "Even got my Colt back."

"What's Thaxter going to do when he finds you gone?" Canyon asked.

"There's not much he can do—not now, at least. He can't risk sending a squad after me. It'll be dawn soon and the Cheyenne might see them. That'd blow his whole scheme. He has to go on just as he planned," Fargo said.

The circle of wagons appeared ahead and Trudy cast a glance at Fargo. "I'll tell Uncle Ben and the others," she offered. "I'll tell them you were right about the major using us."

"You do that," Fargo said, and there was no softening in his face as she let the sidelong glance linger.

"I'm sorry, Fargo," she said. "We should've listened to you. I should have."

"Sorry's a good word," he said grimly. "Only trouble with it is it usually comes too late to help anything much." He slowed and reined up as they reached the wagons and he saw Cy Estes poke his head out of one Conestoga, rifle in hand.

Trudy rode to her wagon, dismounted, disappeared

inside it, and in moments reappeared with Ben Deakens still struggling into suspenders.

Fargo stepped outside the circle of wagons with Canyon beside him.

"Nothing's changed much for them, for all you tried to do," Canyon said. "They know now they've been used, but knowing won't help them any when the Cheyenne attack."

Fargo's lips pulled back in a grimace. "You're right, too damn right, Canyon," he muttered. "Unless I can still figure a way to save their scalps."

"Sometimes things are out of your hands, lad," Canyon said. "You can't turn the world around."

"Maybe not," Fargo said. "I'll sleep on that."

Canyon nodded, took the palomino, and bedded down under one of the wagons.

Fargo stretched out near Trudy's wagon; he lay still on his bedroll and Canyon's words danced inside him. Perhaps it was all beyond anything further he could do. Maybe it had all gone too far now, past retrieving, past anything but waiting. He let his eyes close in weariness and sleep rolled over him as Canyon's words clung: "You can't turn the world around."

10

"I've got it," Fargo gasped out as he sat up straight on the bedroll. "Damn, I've got it."

The morning sun had come out, he saw, but that wasn't what had wakened him so abruptly. Out of the unfathomable reaches of the mind, where thoughts swirled through sleep that never touched the subconscious, it had exploded to snap him awake. He saw Canyon roll from under the wagon to stare at him.

"You said it, friend," Fargo called to him. "Not exactly but enough to trigger it."

"What are you talking about, lad?" Canyon frowned as he rose to his feet.

"You said I couldn't turn the world around," Fargo said as he felt the excitement spiral through him.

"So I did," Canyon agreed.

"And you were right, of course. But I can turn the wagons around," Fargo said, and saw Canyon's stare narrow in thought. "Thaxter won't bring his men up to us, so we'll bring the wagons to him," Fargo said.

"Just like that?" Canyon asked.

"No, it'll be tricky. When we start back, the Cheyenne will attack. I figure they'll attack anyway today," Fargo said. "But this way Thaxter will be following us while we're moving toward him. With any luck, we'll be within ten minutes of him when they attack."

"Thaxter will reach us before the wagons are wiped out," Canyon said. "By God, it could work, except for one thing: what if the Cheyenne attack the minute we start back?"

"They won't. I know the Cheyenne. They're curious and careful. Anything unusual, and they'll hold back to make sure they won't walk into a trap," Fargo said. "I'd guess we can keep them watching and uneasy for at least twenty minutes before they decide to strike."

"Then we'll be twenty minutes closer to Thaxter and he'll be twenty minutes closer to us," Canyon half-chortled. "But he won't have that total surprise he wants, you know. It'll be too soon for that, the Cheyenne too fresh and too alert. It'll knock his whole plan out, unless Strongarrow decides to stay and fight, and it's not likely he'll do that against two full platoons."

"I don't give a damn about Thaxter's plan. All I care about is that the people in those Conestogas have a chance, and this'll give them that," Fargo returned.

"Then let's do it, lad." Canyon laughed and stepped inside the circle of wagons with the big, black-haired man.

Ben Deakens, Trudy beside him, had gathered in a half-circle with the others, and everyone turned to Fargo as he strode toward them.

"Trudy told us," Deakens said. "We owe you an apology. Seems you were right about the major using us, and we figure you're right about Kragg, too."

"Apologies are for yesterday. Today's all that matters now," Fargo said. "I've a plan. No promises, just an outside chance." They nodded with grave faces and he quickly outlined the core of it and nodded understanding when he finished. "The Cheyenne are back in those trees somewhere, watching us right now," Fargo said. "We start back single-file and slow at first. Going back the way we came will make them wonder some. Then, as you roll, the first three wagons pull up three abreast. You hold that for five minutes, then drop back single-file, and the second three wagons spread out three abreast. Hold that for another five minutes and then you all spread out six abreast and stay that way. The Cheyenne will keep watching and wondering, but they won't attack while they're wondering."

"But they will attack," Trudy said.

"Count on it. Soon as they decide that what we're doing doesn't mean anything, they'll come at us. But if we can get fifteen minutes out of it, I'll be happy," Fargo said. "Now let's roll." He turned to the four troopers who had listened from the side. "Soon as the Cheyenne come at us, you hightail for the major. Don't tell him we're close to him. Just tell him the attack's started."

"I understand, sir," the trooper said. "All of it."

Canyon rode beside him as he moved to the front of the wagon train, Trudy on the driver's seat of the lead wagon behind him, her uncle at the reins. After five minutes, he motioned back and the first three Conestogas moved to roll abreast of each other.

Fargo allowed a grim smile. His eyes swept the distant trees along the side of the high plateau as they rode.

"See anything?" Canyon asked.

"No Cheyenne, but they're moving along with us," Fargo said.

"How do you know that?" Canyon asked.

"Watch the leaves along the low branches. You'll see them stirring."

"How do you know it's not a breeze?"

"A wind blows in gusts, turns the bottoms of the leaves up. These leaves aren't turned up. They're just moving along a straight line."

"You're good, lad," Canyon said admiringly. "Thanks for the lesson."

Fargo glanced back, motioned, and the Conestogas

moved in the pattern he'd instructed them to move. Now the first three were in a single file behind the others. He waited, grateful for the way it was going, and finally motioned again and the six wagons drew abreast of each other.

"We've got our fifteen minutes," he said to Canyon. "The rest is borrowed time. By now they're concluding we've been stringing them along. Besides, they can't afford to let us go back much farther."

As if in answer to his words, the line of trees suddenly exploded with racing Indian ponies. The Cheyenne broke into the open in three bands and Fargo turned in his saddle. "Circle your wagons," he yelled, but saw the Conestogas were already beginning to close together in circle. He saw the four troopers streak past him in full gallop and also saw a half-dozen Cheyenne take off after them. But they'd only pursue a few minutes, he knew, and then return to the battle.

The center band of attackers was led by a bare-chested figure with two eagle feathers sticking out of his beaded headband, and Fargo took in a harsh, strong face with black eyes that gleamed with hate. The Cheyenne chief carried an army carbine, he saw, as did half the others.

The wagons completed their circle and Fargo, Canyon at his heels, leapt through the small space between two of the wagons and inside the circle. He saw Ben Deakens and two other men in position, rifles in hand, and the others hurrying to find places of comparative safety, some of the women holding rifles. Trudy was one of them and Fargo leapt from the saddle, yanked the big Sharps from its saddle case, and dropped down beside her. He glanced over to see Canyon had taken up a spot at the tail of one of the other Conestogas. The Cheyenne were racing in a furious circle but just out of range.

"Hold your fire," Fargo called out. He waited and saw the Cheyenne chief wheel his mount, pump his arm up and down, and the braves turned and raced directly at the wagons. When they were close enough, they turned again and began to race in a circle.

"Fire," Fargo yelled, and the fusillade rang out from the wagon.

Only one brave fell to the ground as the others clung low to their ponies, rising only to fire off a volley of shots or arrows. Fargo followed one, waited, and fired, and the Indian went down as his horse raced on. Strongarrow stayed on the perimeter of the attack, Fargo noted, and suddenly the Cheyenne sent half his braves circling in one direction and half in the other. The Trailsman saw the results of the move at once as those at the wagons fired more wildly, their concentration broken. The Cheyenne also began to fire arrows and bullets in clusters, and Fargo saw two of the defenders go down, then another two, one a woman. Some of the others started to go to their aid. "No," Fargo shouted severely. "Stay in place and keep firing."

He turned back to the attackers and saw two suddenly fall from their ponies; he glanced across at Canyon and caught the smile of satisfaction on his handsome ruddy face.

With a shout, the Cheyenne chief again reversed direction of his racing braves and a furious cluster of shots sent still another of the defenders toppling from behind one of the wagons. Fargo glanced across the small circle just as another defender fell on the far side. He saw Trudy's glance of fear as she paused to reload her rifle.

"Where the hell is Thaxter?" Fargo muttered aloud, but kept the rest of his thoughts to himself. The settlers weren't good-enough marksman to inflict any real damage on the fast-racing Cheyenne, and the two opposite rows of attackers were still flustering the defenders. He dropped low, crawled beneath the Conestoga, brought down two more of the Cheyenne, and scooted backward as three arrows slammed into the ground only inches from his head.

He rose on one knee, risked a moment to lean forward between two of the wagons and peer into the distance where he glimpsed the movement on the horizon. He ducked back and caught Canyon's glance.

"Thaxter," Fargo said. He ducked low again to peer out between the spokes of a wagon wheel and saw Strongarrow make a long sweeping motion with one arm. Instantly, the Cheyenne broke off the attack on the wagons and swept forward after their chief.

Canyon rose to come over and stand beside him, and Fargo watched as the chief split his braves into two groups, each moving out from the other. Major Thaxter's troopers were now fully in sight and charging hard. To avoid being outflanked, Thaxter split his force into two columns and sent them after the two Cheyenne bands, who immediately dispersed into fast-moving individual targets.

Fargo spotted the Cheyenne chief just as the man wheeled his horse and flung his arm straight into the air. Instantly, a band of some twenty warriors burst from the tree line. "I'll be dammed," Canyon breathed. "He had a reserve waiting."

As he watched, Fargo saw the major forced to turn his platoon around to meet the new band of attackers while the first group of Cheyenne darted in and out like so many wasps. But Thaxter halted his platoon and Fargo watched the troopers wheel and bring their concentrated firepower to bear on the new attackers. Close to a dozen Cheyenne went down with the first volley, and the others turned and raced away in different directions.

But Fargo saw more than a few blue-uniformed figures prone on the ground as the Cheyenne continued to dart in and out, smartly refusing to try a concentrated attack on the superior firepower of the cavalry platoons. One Cheyenne raced past within range and Fargo brought the Colt up, fired, and the Indian fell sideways from his pony.

"Every little bit helps," Fargo muttered at Canyon's glance.

The Cheyenne's fast-moving tactics were taking their toll, Fargo saw, but Thaxter had settled his men down to concentrated fire instead of fighting the Cheyenne's game by chasing after them. More silent bronzed-skin figures began to litter the ground and Fargo saw Strongarrow, still at the perimeter of the fighting, signal his warriors. As one, they broke off the battle and began to race for the trees.

"After them, dammit," Thaxter shouted. "Don't let him get away." He raced forward as his troopers came around to chase after him, but Strongarrow had reached the tree line and plunged into the thick foliage, his braves scattering in small groups as they followed him.

Fargo watched the major lead his men into the trees until the entire column disappeared from sight.

"The fool. He'll lose more men in there," Canyon spit out.

"I expect he'll come back out, then," Fargo said, and turned to the others, some of whom were sobbing quietly beside still forms. "You go back to Crooked Branch with the platoon," he said.

"Yes." Ben Deakens nodded, his tired eyes even more tired.

"Aren't you coming?" Trudy asked quickly.

"No. Canyon and I have some unfinished business," Fargo said.

"We could wait for you there," Trudy said.

"All right," Fargo said. "If that's an invitation."

"It is," she murmured.

"We've some hard questions for the major," Ben Deakens said. "He shouldn't be allowed to get away with what he tried to do, sacrifice a whole wagon train."

"That's another reason why you have to come back, Fargo," Cy Estes added. "We'll file a formal charge, but we'll need your statement for it. You were the one he arrested and was going to kill when you realized what he was doing."

"I'll stop back," Fargo agreed.

"When the major comes back with his men, I'll tell him it was your idea that kept most of us alive," Trudy said.

Fargo allowed a grim laugh. "He'll say all the right things, but don't believe any of it." He turned and swung onto the pinto, Canyon already waiting on the palomino.

"Come back," Trudy called after him, her deep-blue eyes moist, and he gave her a private nod.

He rode from the circle with Canyon and gestured straight ahead. "We take the trees," Fargo said. "There are a lot of real mad Cheyenne around. They'll be in the tree cover, too, but we won't be such perfect targets if we aren't crossing the plateau out in the open."

Canyon nodded and followed him into the thick woodland and motioned west.

Fargo swung the pinto around and moved through the heavy tree cover. They had gone some hundred yards or so when he halted, his ears picking up the sound of brush being pushed backward. The sound came from deep in the woodland and grew louder quickly. Horses moving through the brush—at least four. Fargo frowned and changed his conclusion. A lot more than four horses, he muttered silently. He swung from the Ovaro and gestured to a thicket of high brush, and Canyon followed him in and dropped to the ground.

The soft scraping of small branches grew louder, and Fargo glimpsed the line of horsemen moving down the hillside, blue uniforms appearing through the foliage. They rode in twos, with the major in front.

"He got away," Thaxter bit out to no one in particular. "The savage bastard got away again. We got to him too soon, goddammit. We didn't have enough surprise in it. Rotten, murdering bastard got away." The major passed within a dozen feet of where Fargo and Canyon were hidden inside the thicket, and he continued to curse and rant in fury as he moved on.

Fargo watched the troops following, young weary faces, some still wearing fear in their eyes. The last ten horses in the line carried troopers lain facedown across their saddles.

Fargo and Canyon remained motionless until the blue line disappeared down through the sloping tree cover, and finally Fargo moved out and climbed back onto the pinto. "I wonder how many more the Cheyenne lost," Canyon said.

"Not as many, not in these forests," Fargo grunted. "That's why they hightailed it in here." He cast a glance at Canyon with a question in his eyes. "How do you figure to find Kragg?" he asked.

"He'll be west and north of here, making good time," Canyon said. "You're the Trailsman. You call it."

"We go west. We ought to be able to pick up his wagon marks. Then we follow north."

"And be careful the Cheyenne don't pick us up," Canyon said. "They've been hurt, even if Strongarrow got away. They'll be on the warpath with an extra vengeance.''

"We might still be lucky. They might take care of Kragg for us," Fargo said.

"Yes, but we won't count on that. Let's ride,'' Canyon said, and sent the palomino forward.

Fargo fell in alongside and rode through the hills. Below, he saw the high plateau come to an end.

"You watch for Cheyenne, I'll watch for wagon tracks," Canyon suggested, and Fargo nodded agreement. He glanced back at the way they had come, their prints clear in the soft, fresh hill soil. Any Cheyenne scout could pick them up. He grimaced and brought his eyes back to scanning the thick wooded terrain.

They had gone some fifteen miles, he guessed, through difficult hill country, and the dusk began to slide across the mountains. It was almost dark when Canyon uttered a cry of triumph and reined to a halt. "There," he said, and Fargo followed his finger, which pointed to the ground. The wagon marks were deep and clear, crossing their path on the way north. Fargo dismounted and knelt by the marks and the hoofprints that all but surrounded them, his fingers moving across them, touching the edges and pressing into the deeper parts.

"Maybe six hours old," he said as he rose, glancing at the darkness now flooding the area. "We'll never trail them by night in these mountains. We'll bed down here and follow, come morning.''

"Sounds good to me. I'm feeling weary," Canyon said. He set out his bedroll as Fargo did the same. "You had a good day, Fargo. You saved a wagon train from being massacred."

"And helped let a Cheyenne chief off the hook. I'm

not particularly happy about that," Fargo answered as he stretched out.

"It had to be. It was part of the price," Canyon said. "I hope it goes as well for me tomorrow. Good night, lad."

" 'Night," Fargo murmured, and sleep swept quickly over his long, muscled frame as he pushed away the moment of uneasiness that stabbed at him. He slept soundly and the night remained still.

When the morning sun came over the high peaks, Fargo woke and saw Canyon already dressed.

"It's called being anxious," the Irishman said. "Like a kid the night before Christmas."

"I know the feeling," Fargo said, dressing hurriedly. He found a stand of wild red grapes for breakfast and swung in behind the wagon tracks that were clear and deep.

They rode up the steep mountainsides and saw where the wagon had trouble climbing. At one spot, the outriders had to dismount and help push until the ground leveled off some. But the tracks grew fresh and it was just after noon that he halted and swung from the horse. "We walk from here. They could be stopped. We don't want to stumble in on them," he said.

"No, that's the last thing we want," Canyon agreed.

The terrain had grown thick with brush and hackberry again and only a narrow trail let the wagon move through. Half the gunslingers had swung in behind, Fargo saw, the other half in front. He moved on up the narrow path, Canyon at his side and the horses following behind when he suddenly halted, pressed one hand on the big redheaded man's shoulder.

"Listen," he said, waiting another moment until the sound came again, the creak of wagon wheels. Not more than a hundred yards ahead, Fargo estimated.

He motioned to the trees to the right as he silently climbed into the saddle. Canyon followed him from the narrow pathway and up a steep incline. He moved the Ovaro forward, paralleled the narrow path below, and suddenly came in sight of the wagon, wrapped tightly in canvas as Canyon had described. The six gunhands were riding herd on the wagon, three on each side and Kragg driving.

"Four for me and three for you," Canyon muttered. "I think we can do it."

"It'll have to be fast and dirty," Fargo said, and Canyon looked uncomfortable.

"I know, and that bothers me. It goes against my sense of proper behavior," the red-haired man said.

"Too cold-blooded?" Fargo smiled.

"Yes. I always like to give a man the chance to do the right thing for himself," Canyon said. "One can be a gentleman about anything, even an ambush."

"That's why the world is full of dead gentlemen," Fargo said blandly, but he understood the emotions that churned inside Canyon O'Grady. He wasn't much for cold-blooded killing, either, but he wasn't one for being a fool. "You think they'd give you a chance if things were turned around?"

"Two wrongs don't make a right," Canyon said with a touch of the preacher in his voice.

"Amen," Fargo said. "Your show."

Canyon grimaced again and started to move the palomino down the slope toward the wagon below, and Fargo unholstered the big Colt. Canyon halted when they were a dozen yards from the men and a few feet in front of the wagon. Fargo moved the Ovaro sideways along the slope until he was slightly behind the riders. He halted and raised the Colt.

O'Grady raised his hand to him, his own six-gun

ready, Fargo saw. "You're under arrest, Kragg," Canyon called out. "Everybody drop their guns."

Fargo uttered a grim snort as he saw the six gunslingers pause for only a moment and then yank their guns out as they spurred their mounts forward. He had one in his sights already and he fired. The man seemed to buck in the saddle before toppling to the ground. Fargo fired again, two shots so close together that might have been one. And two of the gunslingers went down, one hitting the back of the wagon as he fell, the other landing almost on top of him.

Canyon's six-gun was exploding also, and Fargo saw two more of the riders go down. The third one had wheeled his horse and started to race back down the passageway. Fargo fired and heard Canyon's gun go off at the same time. The two bullets slammed into the fleeing gunslinger and the man pitched forward across the neck of his horse, hung there for an instant, and then fell to one side. He left a smear of red along the galloping horse's neck.

Fargo's attention returned to the wagon below. Kragg was spurring the horses on, trying to flee in an almost laughably futile attempt. Canyon sent the palomino down the rest of the slope and raced alongside the wagon. Kragg pulled the wagon to a halt when he saw the Colt Army Model pointed at the side of his head.

"Get down," Canyon ordered as Fargo rode up and Kragg stepped to the ground. "Your gun," Canyon said, and Kragg drew a short-barrel Smith & Wesson Volcanic cartridge repeater model from his belt and tossed it on the ground. Canyon dismounted, picked up the pistol, and threw it into the trees. He stepped to the canvas on the wagon and used a hunting knife to cut one corner open. The tightly packed stacks of bonds came into view at once and he laughed as he turned to

Kragg. "The best-laid plans of mice and men . . ." he began, and let the rest trail off.

Kragg stared at him with his nervous eyes suddenly grown still, his face dour.

"What now?" Fargo asked.

"Tie him up, just so's I don't have to worry about him, then turn the wagon around and drive out of these damned Indian-infested mountains. There's a U.S. marshal's office back in Whitewater. I'll turn him in there."

"And the bonds?" Fargo asked.

"They'll be shipped back to the treasury office for the southwest region. I might even have to play shepherd for them," Canyon said.

Fargo was about to say something more when he halted and saw Canyon freeze in place also as they both heard the sound of horses moving fast through the trees. "Behind the wagon," Fargo snapped, and he followed Canyon with Kragg hurrying along.

"Cheyenne?" Canyon wondered aloud.

"Maybe, but they're making more noise than Cheyenne would make normally," Fargo said. He'd just finished the reply when the blue-uniformed riders burst into the open, Major Howard Thaxter in the lead. Fargo saw ten troopers fan out behind him all with carbines ready to fire.

"Come out from behind there, Fargo," the major barked, and Fargo rose and stepped into view. Canyon followed with him and Kragg tentatively showed himself. "I'm taking you back. Your friend there, too," Thaxter said. "You're under arrest."

11

"What the hell for?" Fargo demanded.

"For interfering in a military operation," Major Thaxter snapped, a satisfied look on his face.

"I saved a wagon train from being massacred, dammit," Fargo protested.

"You see it your way. I see it mine," Thaxter said icily. "We'll let a military court decide." He motioned to two of his troopers. "Get their guns," he said, and the two cavalrymen dismounted and came forward at once.

Fargo eyed the other carbines trained on him and decided against a rash move. Besides, he'd no wish for a shoot-out with ten young troopers obeying orders. He turned his Colt over to them and saw Canyon hand them the ivory-gripped six-gun.

"I'm a United States government agent," Canyon said to Thaxter. "I've credentials to prove it." He gestured to Kragg. "This man was trying to escape with a half-million dollars of treasury bonds."

Thaxter fastened him with a sneer. "I wouldn't believe anything either of you said, and I wouldn't be taken in by fake credentials," he answered.

"You mean you don't want to believe it," Canyon said.

"Get on your horses. I'm taking you back," the major said.

Canyon gestured to Kragg. "What happens to him?" he protested.

"I don't give a damn about him," Thaxter snapped, and Fargo watched the smile spread across Kragg's face.

"That man's my prisoner, dammit," Canyon shouted.

"Not anymore he isn't," Kragg shrugged.

"Thank you, Major. What he said was all a pack of lies," Kragg called out.

"Don't thank me, mister. You're nothing to me. Just stay out of my way," Thaxter answered contemptuously, and watched Fargo and Canyon take the saddle. "Four men in back of them. Three on each side," he ordered his troopers. "They make one wrong move, shoot them."

His troopers obeyed at once and Thaxter started to lead the way back down the narrow passage. Along with Canyon, Fargo heard the creak of the wagon wheels as Kragg drove off.

"Dammit to hell," Canyon swore, bitterness wrapping each word, and he glanced at the troopers surrounding him and then at Fargo.

"We've got other problems," Fargo murmured. "You don't think we'll ever reach that military court, do you?"

"Of course I do, lad, and I believe in the tooth fairy, too," Canyon muttered darkly.

"He must have taken off after us the minute he got back to the wagons," Fargo said. "He picked up our tracks and just followed."

"He had to. Without you, no one on the wagon train can make it stick," Canyon put in.

"We've got to wait and pick the right moment," Fargo said.

"If we can find one before he does," Canyon growled.

Fargo grunted agreement as they rode on. His eyes were boring into Thaxter, who rode a half-dozen yards in front of him.

It happened with such blinding suddenness that Fargo heard the gasp escape his lips. The first arrow hurtled into the center of the major's back with such force that even the feathers almost disappeared. Thaxter's arms flew up into the air as he dropped the reins, and the gasped groan that rose from him was cut short as a second arrow went through one side of his neck and out the other. He sat as if pinned to an invisible board in midair before he toppled from his mount.

His fall galvanized the stunned troopers, but not before two more fell from their horses, arrows piercing their chests. Fargo and Canyon dived from their horses at once, both rolling into the brush, and the Trailsman twisted to avoid another trooper who fell with two arrows through his stomach. Fargo seized the fallen man's carbine as the Cheyenne broke into sight from the slope. He fired, spraying shots in a short arc, and had the satisfaction of seeing three of the attackers go down. He glimpsed Strongarrow race along the line of trees, dart into cover as he flung a lance that smashed through another of the troopers, hurtling into the soldier's chest. Fargo's shot at the Cheyenne chief missed, and he saw Canyon reach out and pull one of the carbines to him.

Most of the remaining troopers had taken cover in the brush near where Fargo crouched beside Canyon. "Hold your fire," Fargo said. "Don't shoot till you get a good target." The Cheyenne had fallen silent and Fargo lowered his voice as he spoke to the troopers. "Watch the sides," he said, and saw the soldiers half-turn to cover both ends of the brush. The silence exploded with war whoops as the Cheyenne erupted, and Fargo glimpsed the bronzed forms racing back and forth in the tree cover in front of them. "Hold your fire," he said again. "Keep watching the sides."

"They're putting on a show to draw our fire," Canyon said, and Fargo nodded as the Cheyenne raced back and forth again.

Suddenly, from both ends of the thicket, two more groups of attackers burst forward—but no decoy maneuvers, now, as they charged, guns firing.

One of the troopers near Fargo went down, but the others, alerted and ready, poured a heavy return fire at their attackers. Fargo saw three of the Cheyenne fall at one end, four at the other, and the Indians darted away as they broke off the attack.

Fargo looked down at the fallen trooper near where he crouched. "You hurt bad, boy?" he asked.

"My shoulder, sir," the trooper said.

"Just stay quiet," Fargo muttered, and met Canyon's glance. "They're deciding their next move," he said, and turned back to the troopers. "Don't fire at noise," he reminded them, and reloaded his Colt. He rested on one knee, his jaw tight.

Suddenly, from almost opposite him, the trees exploded with a fusillade of shots and arrows. The Trailsman ducked low and yelled at the thin line of troopers, "Hold fire. They're laying down a barrage for something," he said.

The movement to his right caught his eye and he raised his head enough to see the two near-naked forms spring from the tree cover, seize the lifeless form of the major, and pull it into the trees. The fusillade instantly came to a halt.

Fargo stayed unmoving as he listened to the sound of hoofbeats racing away through the woodland. He rose, holstered his Colt, and stepped from the high brush. "It's over," he said. "They got what they wanted." He watched the troopers slowly regain their feet and Canyon stand up with a grim sigh.

"They've been hurt, but the mountains are still theirs. They'll lick their wounds and hang their trophies high,"

Canyon said. There was no need for him to spell it out more clearly.

Fargo's gaze swept the tired young faces before him. "He was your commander, but he didn't command himself. He let himself become twisted inside, eaten away by ambition and obsessed by winning. He made a mockery of his uniform. I can't feel sorry for him. You shouldn't, either," he said.

Canyon's voice cut in, a reminder. "We've still some unfinished business, friend," the redheaded man said.

"Yes," Fargo answered, his eyes still on the remaining troopers. "Go on back. I think you'll make it without any more trouble from the Cheyenne. You'll catch up to the Conestogas. Take them back to town."

"Yes, sir," one of the troopers said, and the others followed him to their mounts.

Canyon strode to the palomino and Fargo swung onto the Ovaro.

"After you, friend." Fargo grinned and Canyon sent the palomino into a gallop. Fargo stayed on his heels as they rode up the narrow passageway, crested a rise, and leveled off to see still another ridge ahead. But the wagon wheels continued on and Fargo suddenly slowed his horse as he pointed past the top of the ridge. A thin column of gray smoke rose straight up in a windless sky.

With a curse, Canyon spurred the palomino forward and took the top of the ridge at a full gallop. Fargo, at his heels, charged over the top and yanked the Ovaro to a halt as, only a dozen yards ahead in a small clearing, the wagon and its contents burned into charred embers. Kragg lay on the ground, four arrows in his thin frame, and four Cheyenne warriors stopped pulling at his clothes to turn at the unexpected interruption.

Two had rifles and they reacted instantly.

Fargo flung himself from the Ovaro and glimpsed

Canyon diving from the palomino. The Trailsman hit the ground as he yanked the Colt from its holster, and he half-rolled, came up on one knee to see the nearest brave charging straight at him. The Indian fired the rifle again and Fargo dived forward. He felt the blast of air as the bullet passed but a fraction over his head. He tried to bring the Colt up, but the Indian, using the rifle as a club now, swung, and Fargo gasped in pain as the barrel of the gun crashed into his forearm. He felt the Colt drop from his fingers as they turned numb instantly. He rolled, twisted, and avoided a kick from the Cheyenne's moccasined foot. He managed to get his other arm out, smashed it against the Indian's ankle, and the brave went down on one knee.

Fargo threw a looping left hook that crashed into the Indian's jaw as, dimly, he heard at least six shots explode. The Cheyenne staggered back and Fargo pushed to his feet. The numbness was growing less in his right arm and he rushed at his foe. The Indian recovered and, with a roaring, guttural sound, dived forward, hands outstretched to close around his opponent's neck.

Fargo swung the left again, but the Indian's diving charge took the blow on his chest and Fargo felt the man's hands close around his neck. He tried to bring his right arm up but the numbness was still there and he felt the weakness in his arm. The brave brushed his arm aside and pressed Fargo backward, his fingers closing tighter around his foe's neck.

Fargo felt the breath immediately growing harsh inside his throat, and with a desperate effort, he brought both fists into the Indian's stomach.

The brave grunted as a rush of air spewed from his mouth and his grip around Fargo's neck loosened for an instant. But an instant was all the Trailsman needed: he flung himself from the Indian, half-rolled, and kicked out backward with all the strength in his legs. The blow slammed into the Cheyenne's groin and the red man fell back in pain. As Fargo grabbed hold of the rifle on the ground, he heard another shot but he had no time to see what it meant as the Indian began to rise again.

Fargo charged forward, the stock of the carbine held in front of him as though it were a lance. Using all the strength of his powerful shoulder muscles, he drove it into the Cheyenne's jaw and heard the shattering of bone. The Indian fell back and lay still.

Fargo spun on one knee as he scooped his Colt from the ground. He felt a trace of the numbness still in his hand, but he saw Canyon O'Grady standing, wiping a small trickle of blood from his forehead, six-gun in hand, and the other three Cheyenne on the ground in the awkward positions of the dead.

"I was lucky. I got two of them right away," Canyon said.

Fargo's eyes went to the wagon, where only small bits of charred paper still remained under the burned canvas.

"It's all right," Canyon said, answering the question in his eyes. "They can burn up and there'll be no loss. It's only if he'd cashed them in that the government would have to pay on them and he'd have his half-million in stolen money. This way they won't be cashed in and they'll have the serial numbers of each bond when they've finished checking. They can just issue new ones."

Fargo's eyes went to Kragg's arrow-riddled form. "The best-laid plans, even with a second chance . . ." he said wryly.

"Well put, lad," Canyon chortled.

Fargo glanced at the four Cheyenne on the ground.

"They weren't with Strongarrow. They were probably just a scouting party he ran into," Fargo said.

"No matter," Canyon said. "But it seems the Cheyenne have done us both a favor, not that they planned it that way." Fargo allowed a grim laugh and his eyes met O'Grady's appraising gaze. "You're a man after my own heart, Fargo," the big redheaded man said.

"You're a good man yourself, O'Grady," Fargo said. "Where do you go now?"

"I've still a report to turn in. Maybe we'll be meeting again."

"I'd like that," Fargo said, and clasped Canyon O'Grady's outstretched hand. He waited as the big man with the roguish face and the fast gun swung onto the copper-sheen palomino, waved back again to him, and rode on down the other side of the ridge.

Fargo pulled himself onto the Ovaro and rode slowly back along the narrow passage. He made his way down through the mountains of the Wind River Mountains. He'd promised Trudy he'd stop back, and he had the definite feeling it was a promise he'd enjoy keeping.

It was night when he reached Crooked Branch after another day's ride down through the mountains. He found the Conestogas camped outside the town behind the stockade walls. He halted, swung to the ground, and though most of the other wagons were dark and silent, he saw a lamp burning low inside Trudy's wagon. He moved closer to the wagon and was almost at the tailgate when she suddenly came outside and stepped to the ground. She didn't see him, her eyes lifted to the half-moon in the blue velvet sky. She wore a nightgown that was both filmy yet proper and lay lightly against the very high, very round breasts.

"Waiting for someone?" he asked softly, and Trudy whirled, black hair tossing, and her eyes grew wide.

152

She was in his arms with one long half-stride, half-leap. Her lips found his, soft pressure that quickly increased, became full and hungering. "Now, that's the kind of greeting I like," he murmured when she finally pulled away.

"The troopers caught up to us. They told us what happened," Trudy said. "I wondered if you'd bother coming back now."

"I told you I would," he said with a trace of reprimand in his voice.

Her eyes searched his face. "Maybe it's best it ended this way," she ventured.

"Yes, maybe it's best. Thaxter will go down a hero in the official records, and most of you are alive. I'll leave it that way. There's nothing to be gained now by going further," Fargo said.

She came to him again and her lips found his mouth once more. "Not for that," she agreed, clung to him, and he felt the soft warmth of her breasts through the filmy material.

"I'll find a place tomorrow," Fargo said.

"No, tonight," Trudy murmured, and he felt a moment of surprise.

"Never say no to a lady or a good drink." He shrugged and lifted her in his arms and onto the saddle of the pinto. He swung up behind her and moved the horse forward, up a low hill, and found a spot where a pair of red cedar offered a dark and leafy cover and a mat of wavy broom moss a soft bed.

"Where's your friend?" Trudy asked as he lifted her to the ground.

"On his way to turn in a report." Fargo smiled. "And if I know Canyon O'Grady, he'll find himself a pair of warm arms and willing lips along the way."

Trudy came down on her knees beside him as he stretched out on the soft moss. "You've already found that," she murmured, and her hands went to the top of the nightgown.

She pulled a string and the neck of the garment fell open to reveal the very round, very high breasts that, even without a blouse to hold them firm, retained their shape. He took in their loveliness, cream-white and beautifully round, each tipped by a light-pink nipple that lay almost flat inside a light-pink circle.

She watched him shed clothes and he heard the tiny gasp as her eyes roamed across his smoothly muscled body. He reached out, hands curling around the high, round breasts. They were firmly soft, smooth, and warm, and he ran his thumbs gently across the flat nipples and Trudy's lips opened and her head fell back, the thick black hair cascading down her back. Gently, he brought his lips to one creamy, firm mound and kissed it gently, then drew the light-pink tip in while his tongue circled the tiny nipple.

"Oh, oh, God," Trudy gasped out as she fell back onto the moss. He felt the small tip begin to grow less flat, take on a new, pliant firmness as he caressed it with his tongue. Trudy's hands dug into his shoulders, and when he drew away, she wriggled herself free of the rest of the nightgown, and Fargo took in a deep spring of rib under the round breasts that narrowed into a small waist. Below it, a soft abdomen covered with enough flesh to give it a sensual outward curve led down to a black triangle that held its own dark wildness. Full-curved, smooth thighs followed, leading into dimpled knees and lovely long calves. Trudy Deakens was a rarity, a young woman as lovely without clothes as with them, not a blemish on her, not a line or sag anywhere, all the vibrant beauty of youth still holding fast to her.

She half-rose, pushed her breasts up to him again, and he took each in turn, gently pulling, caressing, sucking, and Trudy cried out in delight as her hands moved up and down the back of his neck. He let his lips move down along her body, a delicate trail, and Trudy cried out with a sudden burst of anticipation as his hand closed over the black triangle, fingers moving through the curled filaments of pleasure and down farther.

"Aaaah . . . ah, ah," Trudy half-cried, half-gasped, and his hand moved down, cupped around the dark entrance, and he felt the moistness on her inner thighs already. "Oh, God, yes, yes . . . oooooh," Trudy murmured as his hand touched, explored, felt the succulent softness of her inner lips, and Trudy's voice rose in an arching cry.

Her hands clasped his hips, slid around to his buttocks, fingers digging into soft flesh as her hips began to writhe. "Take me, Fargo, oh, God, take me," she half-sobbed as he continued to stroke and caress her dark and secret places, and when he rose, let his throbbing, hot maleness press through the dark triangle, her wailing cry of wanting spiraled into the night. He moved, touched the wet portal, and Trudy lifted her hips for him, offering, entreating, the body crying out in its own language, and he moved again, brought himself to the fervid opening. "Aaaaaah . . . aiiii," Trudy cried out, and when he thrust slowly forward through the warm channel, her cry rose, became a scream of pleasure, and suddenly she was lifting, pushing, pumping with him, the screams becoming harsh grunting sounds as she sought ecstasy.

His mouth came down to pull on the round, firm breasts and he felt the flat tips now risen, quivering for his tongue. Trudy's grunting, half-growling cries grew faster, deeper, louder, until suddenly her fingers dug hard into his hips and he saw the black hair toss from side to side. "Oh, my God," Trudy gasped out. "I . . . I . . . Oh, God, now, now . . . it's now."

He felt her quivering against his pulsating strength, soft vise of ecstasy, her thighs locked around him, then falling open, coming together and falling open again as the tide of absolute pleasure swept through her. Her final scream held in midair as he let himself join with her in that climax that ended too soon yet never really ended, that moment of moments that swept on but stayed forever to seek renewal another time and another place.

Finally Trudy sank back and her arms held his face against her breasts as she drew in deep breaths of despair and satisfaction. He slowly slid from her and she gave a tiny gasp; he lay beside her, his hand cupping one round, creamy mound. He let her bring her body back to order and she finally pushed onto one elbow, breasts dipping down only slightly.

"Am I still a package of trouble?" she slid at him.

"There's all kinds of trouble," he said blandly.

"Damn you," she flared, and sank her teeth into his shoulder. She drew back, sat up, and looked deliciously lovely. "There's something else I have to tell you," she said. "Uncle Ben and the others will be wanting to talk to you, come morning. They want to go on and they want you to take them, your way, the long way."

His eyes held her in a studied glance. "Anything else?"

"That's why I wanted this tonight."

"Why?"

"So's you wouldn't get the wrong idea. I didn't want it to seem like a thank you or a reward or a bribe. I wanted it to be for itself. I don't know what to call it, really," Trudy said.

"How about a promise?"

She thought for a moment. "Yes, a promise. I like that. A promise." She paused and searched his chiseled face. "What are you going to tell them?"

"I'll take them through, my way," he said.

"They don't have much money, but I know they'll chip in to pay you," Trudy said.

"No, Kragg already paid me. He'll pick up the tab. Seems sort of poetic justice." Fargo chuckled. Canyon O'Grady would approve, he laughed silently. He pulled Trudy against him and she came at once, all softness and warmth.

"What are you thinking?" she said at the smile that touched his lips.

"The long way will be the best way," he said.

"Oh, yes . . . definitely."

He laughed again silently. Trudy had turned from a package of trouble to a package of pleasure. The world had its own ways of rewarding a man for a job well done.

LOOKING FORWARD!
The following is the opening section from the next novel in the exciting *Trailsman* series from Signet:

The TRAILSMAN #90
MESABE HUNTDOWN

Late August, 1859, northern Minnesota
just below the Rainy River at
the back edge of Crow country . . .

The lone horseman rode swiftly, his bronze-skinned, near-naked form glistening in the last of the day's sun. His black hair, heavy with fish oil, flowed back in the wind, held in place by a Crow headband. A short bow and a rawhide quiver of arrows were slung over his shoulder, a tomahawk tucked into the waistband of the breechclout he wore, his only garment of clothing. The sun began to drop over the horizon as he rode through stands of red cedar and hemlock and the house came into view.

He rode down toward where the structure rose in the center of a small clearing. A road led to the clearing, but he came down from the low hills and saw the three guards on their horses at the edge of the tree line, each man carrying a rifle. They were, as they had been the day before, some thirty yards apart.

The bronze-skinned horseman moved the pinto to where the trees thinned and the three guards would see him. They reacted immediately, one bringing his gun around to fire off two hasty shots that went wild. The Crow warrior sent the pinto moving in and out of the trees. His narrowed eyes were on the house. He saw the door fly open and two more men rush out, both with revolvers in hand.

One of the three guards on horseback called out at once. "It's that goddamn Indian again," he said. "The one who was here yesterday."

"Forget him," one of the men who'd come from the house rasped. "He's not the one we have to look out for."

"He makes me nervous. What's he doing here?" the man on the horse asked.

"Maybe he's looking to steal some horses or maybe he just wants some coup stories to tell around the tribal fire," the other man said. "Kill him if he comes too close. Meanwhile, keep your eyes on that damned road." He turned, motioned to the man beside him, and both strode back into the house and pulled the door shut.

The Crow warrior turned his pinto and raced back in front of the three guards in the tree line, letting them glimpse him for the briefest of moments before disappearing back into the trees again. He halted suddenly to peer out at the horizon where the sun had vanished and dusk began to roll over the land, and his eyes went to the house again. A grim smile broke the stonelike impassivity of his chiseled countenance. He had found out what he had wanted to learn. There were five guards, three outside the house and two inside. He waited, motionless, and let the dusk slide across the land while he watched the three outside guards position themselves again in the trees. They stayed on their horses, remaining some thirty yards apart, still visible in the lowering light of the day, each clearly able to watch the small road that led to the clearing and the house.

Before the light faded completely, the Crow warrior moved his pinto down closer to the three outside guards, again letting the animal crash through the brush as he raced along the line where the three men sat their horses. He allowed a fleeting glimpse of himself in the last of the light.

"It's that damn Indian again," he heard one of the men call out. He swerved the horse and disappeared deeper into the woods. He continued riding and let the sound of the horse hurrying trot drift back to the three men until, out of hearing range, he halted and slid from the animal's back. He lowered himself to the ground, relaxed against a red cedar, and let the night grow deeper. Finally, he rose and began to move down the hillside on foot, the pinto following along behind him.

When he neared the line where the three outside guards waited, now shrouded in the blackness of the night, he halted and dropped the rope halter of the pinto over a branch, rested his hand against the horse's neck for a moment, and then moved on alone. On steps silent as a bobcat's prowl, he moved through the trees, each step firm yet feather-light as he passed through brush without rippling a twig and through low branches without disturbing a leaf. Finally, the dark bulk of the nearest guard took shape atop his horse, and as the Crow drew nearer, he took a length of rawhide from the belt of his breechclout and twisted the thin strip in his hands.

The guard's attention was focused on the house and

the road just below the slope where he waited, and he was totally unaware of the stealthy figure moving up behind him. But his horse picked up the presence of an intruder in the night, moved, pawed the ground, and snorted air restlessly.

"Shut up and quiet down," the man growled in annoyance. "Damn-fool nag."

A wry smile touched the lips of the bronzed, near-naked figure. The damn fool sat in the saddle, he grunted silently. It was always the mark of a man who didn't pay attention to his mount. But the stealthy figure moved forward and thanked the spirits for the number of such fools in the world. When he was close enough, the horse still snorting air in alarm; the stealthy figure struck with a motion instant as a firefly's light and fluid as an arc of water. In one motion, he sprang and looped the length of rawhide around the man's neck, and the man came out of the saddle without more than a faint, hissed gasp.

The Crow caught the figure in midair and noiselessly lowered it to the ground. Unconscious, the man still breathed as the Crow pulled the length of rawhide away from his victim's throat. It would be at least ten minutes before enough oxygen returned to the man's brain to bring him out of unconsciousness.

The Indian hurried on, once again on swift, silent steps. The second guard came into sight under the light of the moon that filtered through the thick tree cover. He, too, had his gaze focused on the house and the road below.

The Crow warrior moved silently around to the front of the guard, whose horse lifted its head, ears held straight as it picked up his scent. The powerful, bronze-skinned figure drew the bow from around his shoulders, placed an arrow on the string, and drew the bow back. When he suddenly rose up in front of the guard, the bow was drawn back as far as it would go, the arrow poised to take flight, and he saw the astonishment flood the man's face. It was the instant he had counted on, the numbing moment of surprise that froze the man in place, and when the man snapped himself out of his trance, the arrow was already hissing through the air.

The man reached for his revolver, but he never got the weapon out of the holster as the arrow smashed into his chest, burying itself almost up to the feathers at that short range. The guard grasped at the shaft protruding from his chest even as he toppled backward from his horse. His hands were still curled futilely around the shaft of the arrow as he hit the ground to lay still in one of the brushes.

There was one more, the warrior reminded himself as he moved through the forest. When he came to the third figure, he dropped to one knee. The guard's attention was not riveted on the house or the road. He had plainly paid attention to the sudden restlessness of his horse, and he turned in one direction and then another, peering into the dark of the surrounding trees. A shaft of moonlight caught the glint of the gun in his hand and the Crow's lips drew back in a grimace. Silence was still all-important. A shot would alert those inside the house.

But another arrow wasn't the answer. The guard was moving, and even if it did hit him full force, his finger might tighten on the trigger, and the shot would explode in the night like a cannon's roar. The near-naked figure stayed on one knee and waited, silent as a chuckwalla on a rock. The guard finally stopped turning and brought his horse to a standstill facing the house. But the gun remained in his hand, and only when he finally pushed it into its holster did the Crow warrior rise to his feet. He moved closer to the guard and saw he'd have to come at the man from the side as a thick cluster of buckhorn plantain made any approach from behind impossible. He crept around the thick bushes, halted, measuring distance as he crouched and gathered every fiber of his powerful body. He leapt, a diving upward arc of his body, and the man in the saddle was struck by an arrow made of muscle, bone, and sinew. It smashed into his ribs and sent him flying from his horse. He hit the ground with a grunt of pain.

The Indian was upon him instantly, sinking one knee deep into the man's abdomen while he yanked the gun from its holster. He smashed the butt of the gun down onto the guard's skull, and the man lay still. The Crow rose, tossed the six-gun into the bushes, and turned toward the house in the clearing. Lamplight burned in two of the rooms, the larger in the front of the house and the smaller near the back. He saw one of the guards move past the window in the large room and brought his gaze to the other room. The young woman finally appeared for a moment and then moved out of sight. The Crow warrior darted from the trees to cut across the cleared land around the house. He spied the door at the rear of the building and was at it in half-a-dozen long strides.

He closed his hand around the doorknob and the door came open. He slipped into the house to pause inside a dimly lighted corridor. A lamp burned at the far end of the hallway and he heard the two men talking somewhere around the corner of the hall. He turned and moved on silent steps down to the other end of the corridor to find the room where he had seen the young woman. He'd take her from under their noses in silence if he could, he told himself, and he quickly found the room, the only one with a sliver of light coming from under the door. Once again, he closed a doorknob under one large hand and turned it ever so slowly until the latch came open so softly that even he couldn't hear it.

The young woman sat at a small table at the side of the room, brushing her hair in front of a mirror. The brown hair hung shoulder-length, a fine, gossamer texture to it. Clad only in a white nightgown of a material that fairly shimmered in the lamplight, she had broad, square shoulders and a long waist that widened into full hips. He crossed the room with soundless steps and the young woman didn't know he was there until the reflection of the smooth, powerfully muscled chest suddenly appeared in the mirror.

He saw her stare at the reflection, uncertain whether she was seeing or imagining, and she suddenly spun on the stool to peer at him. Astonishment and terror welled up in her eyes; her lips, red and full, fell open; and the scream began to gather in her throat. The Crow warrior brought his fist downward in a short, clipping blow that landed alongside her jaw. Her eyes rolled back into her head at once and she collapsed as he caught her before she hit the floor.

He lowered her to the floor and glimpsed full, up-turned breasts that partly spilled from one side of the nightgown. He took another moment to scan the room and he pulled a handful of garments from a closet that was partly open; he tossed them into a canvas sack near the bed that took up part of the room. With a quick, almost effortless motion, he scooped the young woman from the floor and tossed her over one shoulder. The sack in his hand, he fled the room and felt the warm softness of her stomach against his shoulder and the smooth roundness of her rear as he held her in place with one hand. He had almost reached the back door when he heard the shout, and he whirled to see one of the two guards had stepped into the corridor.

"Holy Jesus," the man shouted. "It's the goddamn Indian."

The warrior pulled the door open and fled outside as he saw the man yank the six-gun from its holster. He heard the shot splinter the door behind him as he ran into the open, and he knew the guard would charge from the house, six-gun blazing, before he could cross the clear space to the trees. He dropped to one knee against the outer wall of the house and let the girl slide to the ground, and he had the tomahawk in hand, his arm raised, as the guard burst from the back door.

The man halted for an instant as he frowned, his gaze sweeping the cleared land where he had plainly expected to see the fleeing figure. The tomahawk smashed into the side of his face before he had a chance to turn, embedding itself almost to the handle. The man toppled with the front and back of his head almost two halves.

The second guard was following quickly, the Indian realized, and he was racing in a crouch toward the door when the men ran from the house. The second guard halted, stared for a moment at the crumpled figure on the ground, and then, catching the sound of racing footsteps, he whirled, firing as he did. But the Crow had already dived, a low, downward tackle that caught the last guard just below the knees as he felt the bullets pass over his back.

The man went down, still firing, his shots going harmlessly into the air. The warrior reached one long, muscled arm out and caught the man's wrist. He bent it backward and the guard dropped the gun with a curse of pain. But he managed to bring his knee up and sink it into the Indian's abdomen. The Crow fell back for an instant, his grip on the man's wrist coming loose. The guard whirled on the ground, trying to reach his gun. But the big, bronzed figure smashed a fist down on the back of his head. The blow drove the man's face into the ground, and when he tried to lift his head, the Indian seized him by the hair, half-lifted and half-turned him, and smashed a thundering blow into his face. The man fell forward and lay still as the Crow let go of his hair.

He'd be unconscious for more than long enough, the Indian grunted as he returned to the girl, lifted her over his shoulder again, and scooped up the sack of clothes. He moved calmly and quietly into the trees and made his way back to where he'd left the pinto. He placed the girl across the horse's back on her stomach, held the sack by its strap, and climbed onto the horse. He undid the rope halter from the branch and moved unhurriedly away.

He rode north through the trees and kept the young woman in place with one hand. He had left the slope, crossed a low ridge, and moved on when the young woman awoke and he saw her try to lift her head to look up at him. Not ungently, yet firmly, he pushed her head down with one hand and continued to ride northward.

"I'm getting an upset stomach," he heard the girl

say. "Not that you'd understand or give a damn." He rode on and she fell silent and stayed that way except for an occasional oath of discomfort.

He had reached open land before he drew to a halt at the edge of a small lake where a crack willow grew to the very shore in front of a tall stand of pokeweed. He patted the young woman on her round, firm rear and she slid from the horse, landed on her feet and watched him dismount. He motioned to the ground and she lowered herself onto a bed of elf-cap moss, and he glimpsed the combination of fear and defiance in her eyes as he turned his back to her.

He walked to the lake and stepped into the water, glanced back, and saw surprise add itself to the emotions mirrored in her eyes. The Crow warrior immersed himself in the water, executed a quick dive under the surface and came up shaking a cascade of water from himself. He dived again, surfaced, rolled twice in the water, and swam the few yards to the shore. He rose from the water, walked onto the shoreline, every bit as beautifully muscled, but the bronze sheen to his skin had been replaced by a deep tan. The browband gone, his hair, while still black, was no longer flat and heavy with fish oil; it fell in a soft wave.

The young woman stared at him and, for the first time, saw the lake-blue of his eyes. "Damn. You're no Indian," she breathed.

"Go to the head of the class," the big man said.

She stared, her frown of astonishment deepening with each passing moment. "You're him," she breathed. "The one they expected."

"I figured they might be expecting somebody," the big man said.

Her eyes narrowed slightly. "Why'd you expect that?"

"Your Uncle Cyrus isn't the kind to keep anything quiet. I knew he'd brag, and men are quick to sell information," the big man answered.

Her lips pursed in thought for a moment. "So you came as an Indian," she murmured.

"It let me get close enough to see, count noses, and find out what I wanted to know."

"And they'd dismiss you as an Indian looking to steal some horses, maybe," she finished. "Very clever. You've a real name, I presume."

"Fargo . . . Skye Fargo. Some call me the Trailsman," the big man said. He let his gaze take in the young woman properly for the first time. Tall, slightly longish breasts, but with nicely upturned cups that pressed two tiny points into the silk of the nightgown. A narrow and long waist and long thighs under the gown, she had fine, gossamerlike brown hair in an even-featured face, full red lips, a short nose, and eyes so light brown they were almost beige. She was dammed attractive, he decided, yet there was an edge of hardness in her face, a mirror of something inside.

"No need for me to ask your name. You're Julie Hudson," Fargo said, and she answered with a half-smile. "Where's your stepfather?" he questioned.

"Away for a few days," the young woman said.

"We won't be waiting," Fargo said, and walked to the thick cluster of pokeweed, reached in, and drew out a bundle of clothes, then a saddle and a bedroll. "I'm going to get some sleep," he said.

"Like that?" Julie Hudson asked, eyes flicking to the wet breechclout he still wore as his only clothing.

"Why not? It's easy to get used to and it makes for

comfortable sleeping." Fargo laughed. "You can sleep on the moss or I'll give you a blanket."

"The moss. It's a warm night," she said, and he saw her frown as she watched him take the lariat from around the saddle horn and walk toward her with it. "What's that for?"

"So's I can get some sleep without worrying about you," Fargo said. "You see, maybe you don't mind going back to your uncle, but maybe you do. He never made that clear."

"What if I told you I wouldn't try to run?" Julie Hudson asked.

Fargo smiled affably. "Wouldn't make any difference, honey."

Her beige eyes held him in a studied glance. "You don't take any chances, do you?"

"No more than I have to." Fargo smiled and looped the lariat around her left wrist and then tied the other end around his. He walked some ten feet away from her and stretched out on the soft moss. "I'm a very light sleeper," he said, the pleasant matter-of-fact tone a thin disguise for the warning in his words. He watched the young woman settle herself on the moss, her movements smoothly graceful, and she lay down with her back toward him.

"Good night," she murmured, and he grunted a reply with his eyes closed.

The soft lapping of the water against the shore was a soothing sound that brought sleep quickly.

Fargo stayed asleep through the night, waking only when he felt a tug at his wrist. But he saw it was only the girl turning onto her back.

When he woke with the first rays of the dawn sun, Julie Hudson still slept, the silk nightgown up high enough to reveal a long, lovely calf. Fargo rose, untied the rope around his wrist, and took off the breech-clout. He stuffed it into the bottom of his saddlebag and washed with the lake water before donning trousers and gun belt. The girl still lay asleep so he sat down near the water, leaned back on his elbows, and let thoughts drift back to the events that had brought him here.

Cyrus Reiber had come to him after he'd completed a trailblazing drive for Ted Wilks from Dodge City up to South Dakota Territory through too much Sioux country. "I'm told you're the very best and I need the very best," Reiber had told him at their first meeting in a saloon just over the border in Minnesota Territory. He had run a hand through thinning brown hair and offered the kind of money only a fool would turn down. "Meet me at Rock Table in a week and I'll give you the details," Reiber had said. "That's just below Rainy River."

"A week." Fargo had nodded and pocketed the money. He'd taken his time and relaxed on the ride north through Minnesota and found Cyrus Reiber waiting for him at the saloon in Rock Table. The man had consumed one or two whiskeys while waiting, and his somewhat bulbous nose had taken on the red flush of veins long accustomed to alcohol.

Cyrus Reiber, medium height, thin of build, had a garrulous quality to him that made him take a spell before he got into the heart of what he had in his mind. Fargo patiently let the man order another round of drinks.

"It's my niece, Julie Hudson," Cyrus Reiber finally said between sips of whiskey. "I want you to get her and bring her back to me."

"Why?" Fargo asked crisply.

"Because she's supposed to be with me," Reiber said with some indignation.

"Why?" Fargo repeated, unfazed by the man's reaction.

"Because her real pa left instructions that I was to take care of Julie if anything happened to her ma."

"Where is she now?"

"Her stepfather, Tom Colson, has her," the man said.

"Maybe you'd better start at the beginning," Fargo suggested, and Cyrus Reiber sat back after downing his drink.

"Julie Hudson's real pa died when she was about seven or eight years old. This Tom Colson came along and married her ma, and Julie lived with them. Colson's a no-good fourflusher, but I didn't make a fuss. I thought it was best for Julie to stay with her ma, but I kept an eye on her," Cyrus said. "But when her ma died two years ago, Colson refused to let me take over Julie. He kept moving from place to place with her. God knows what he's filled her head with about me. But I paid a lot of money for information and I know where he has her now. I want you to bring her back to me. It's what her real pa, Frank Hudson, said he wanted to happen."

Fargo had listened carefully, turned Reiber's words in his mind. "You know where she is. Doesn't seem you need a trailsman to get her."

"She'll be under guard. Only a man with your skills can get to her. But that's only the first part. After you get her, there'll be plenty more that sure as hell will need a trailsman," Reiber had answered. "That's why I'm paying you the kind of money I am."

Fargo recalled how he had nodded agreement and had set out on the first leg of his task. He recalled how he'd kept thinking of Cyrus Reiber's whiskey-inspired loquaciousness and knew it was more than likely he'd bragged about hiring someone to get his niece back. It was that certainty that had led him to disguise himself as Crow warrior. He was glad for it now: they had definitely been expecting him. He snapped thoughts off as the young woman woke and rubbed sleep from her eyes as she sat up.

In the first, relaxed, unwary moments of waking, she seemed softer, the hard edge gone from her face.

"Get dressed. We've riding to do," Fargo said.

"I'd like to wash in the lake first," she said.

"Be my guest."

"Not with an audience."

"I'm not an audience," Fargo said chidingly. "Your Uncle Cyrus sent me to fetch you, remember?"

"He didn't send you to ogle," she returned tartly.

He shrugged. "It's against my principles not to look."

"What principles?" she half-sneered.

"One of them is never turn your back on beauty," he said, and smiled pleasantly.

"Thanks for the compliment," she said.

"Don't mention it," he said cheerfully.

"Nevertheless, make an exception this time," she said firmly.

He shrugged again. "This time," he said, and turned away.

He heard her go into the lake, and when he looked again, she was swimming and turning in the water. He caught a glimpse of long legs and graceful movements. He took a towel from his saddlebag, tossed it on the shore, and turned his attention to saddling the Ovaro.

She finally emerged, dried herself, and dressed. When he finished tightening the cinch, he turned and saw her in a black skirt and a yellow shirt, looking very attractive, but the edge of hardness had returned to her face.

He motioned to the magnificent Ovaro with the jet-black front and hind quarters and the gleaming white midsection, and she climbed into the saddle. She sat very straight as he swung up behind her, but a firm yet soft rear nonetheless pressed against his legs.

"I prefer riding this way," she commented, and he laughed.

"Tell me about your Uncle Cyrus. What's he got against your stepfather?" Fargo asked as he sent the pinto northward across Minnesota Territory.

"I don't really know. I guess he thinks Tom's not a good influence for me."

"That true?" Fargo queried.

She shrugged. "I don't know."

"He's been living with your ma and you for a long time. You've got to have some idea on that," Fargo pressed.

"He was away a lot," the young woman said.

Fargo felt the small furrow cross his brow as he pushed another remark at Julie Hudson. "Cyrus told me he kept an eye on you over the years," he said.

"I guess you could say that," she answered, and Fargo felt the furrow dig deeper. She'd given him only bland, careful answers on everything he'd asked, almost as though she feared to say anything more.

He broke off asking her further questions and spurred the Ovaro through the gently rolling hillsides until he stopped at another small lake to let the horse rest.

Julie Hudson sat down at the water's edge, cooled her wrists in the water, and finally leaned back on her elbows and let her eyes sweep the terrain. "It's nice here. I like all these lakes. They're all so blue and pure," she commented.

"That's why the Indians named this land Minnesota," Fargo said. "That means the place where the sky is in the land."

She smiled, her longish breasts moving gracefully as she half-turned on one side, her long waist and long legs adding to the smoothness of her every movement.

"Guess you haven't lived long in Minnesota Territory," Fargo remarked.

"We moved around a lot," she said, and he smiled inwardly. It was there again, the answers that were not really answers, never a definite reply.

"Time to ride," he said cheerfully, and she came to her feet with a fluid smoothness that was pretty to see. He set a faster pace when he rode on, and he reached Cyrus Reiber's house just before the sun began to dip down over the horizon.

The man came hurrying out of the front door of his small house as Fargo rode to a halt and swung from the Ovaro. The girl stayed in the saddle and Fargo gestured to her as he smiled. "One niece, signed, sealed, and delivered," he said. "Though it took a little doing."

Cyrus Reiber's eyes stayed fixed on the young woman. "She's not my niece," he said. "She's not Julie."